Meet Julian Penn, Starship Trooper

The Skinnies poured in from everywhere, and the M.I. let them have it. Woczinski's first flamer blast crisped the Skinny civilian with the papers and successfully intimidated the Skinny guards. They dove for cover, firing as they went. Julian violated his own order and lobbed a grenade down the corridor after them, advanced about fifteen feet and crashed through a glass door.

Glass shards showered the Skinny working frantically at a computer in the large office. Julian dove to the floor as laser fire singed the air over his helmet.

"They're coming in behind us," Woczinski shouted.

"No problem," Julian replied, bathing the outside doorway in flaming death.

Shines the Name

"A science fiction fan's dream come true!"

—Gary Gygax

COMBAT COMMAND™

IN THE WORLD OF

ROBERT A. HEINLEIN'S STARSHIP TROOPERS

SHINES THE NAME

BY MARK ACRES

WITH AN INTRODUCTION BY
GARY GYGAX

ACE BOOKS, NEW YORK

This book is an Ace original edition,
and has never been previously published.

SHINES THE NAME

An Ace Book / published by arrangement with
Bill Fawcett & Associates

PRINTING HISTORY
Ace edition / October 1987

INTRODUCTION
by Gary Gygax

No reader hasn't wished to be the protagonist in a book. It is obvious that readers must identify with the main character, or one of them, empathize with that character's emotions, relate to the milieu created by the story, and be caught up in the problems which are posed by the author. The greater the degree of involvement of the reader with the work, the more successful the book. Robert Heinlein is an author who has been creating stories with tremendous reader involvement for many years now. How many is between you and the Good Author. Besides, I have to admit that I've read and collected books by Robert Heinlein since I was a stripling of but 12 years. I, along with millions of others, have wished to be a real-life character involved in the drama of many a novel done by Mr. Heinlein. This very desire helped in the creation of role-playing games.

Consider role-playing games as the antithesis of authored fiction. The role-playing game provides only the operational rules which govern actions in some imagined setting, as well as describing the setting and giving the laws which apply to it. Because a role-playing game involves diverse numbers of individuals there must be no developed heroes and heroines. To become immersed in such a work, each player must create his or her own character as he or she would have it. So too, the particular problems faced and the quests to be undertaken must spring—in part at least—from the dynamics of the players interacting with the game. If there were but one or even a handful of main characters, then which of the players in a group would be him or her? What of the others? How many Lazurus Longs can there be in the world?

Creating characters for adventures in a role-playing game requires a thorough understanding of the game rules, time and effort prior to actual play involvement, and then a great deal of playing and luck to make the character into one of larger-than-life proportions. Along with that goes the creation of problems and quests of the heroic sort for the fledgling game character to solve and attain. The Game Masters of the world have readily adapted their own game settings to encompass published quests. Such scenarios are a step closer to stories, for the scenario details a plot line, antagonists, problems, and a set goal. Players know the game universe and its laws; they provide the characters to operate heroically—they hope—within the setting. In a good book, one never knows the outcome of the story until the end; but it is there, graven in stone. You read to a prescribed conclusion. In a role-playing scenario, however, you interact with the material given, to arrive at an ending which is not predetermined by the author.

Between the novel and the role-playing game lies the "Chosen Path" book. It is part novel, for you have a predetermined character. It is part game, with the milieu defined and the laws set forth for reader interaction. It is part game scenario, because the plot is one of variable paths and the outcome undetermined. The hero can achieve glorious triumph, ignominious defeat, or manage to arrive somewhere in between. The "Chosen Path" book is a "Play Out Your Own Story Line in a Novel", in contrast to a role-playing game which is "Create A Shared Setting for Action-Adventure", and the game scenario which is "See if by Playing You Create an Epic Adventure." Each is separate, interrelated, yet distinct.

Shines the Name is perfect for all of the above. It takes the reader a step closer to role-playing games by involvement and decision. It brings the role-playing game enthusiast into the realms of adventure created by Robert Heinlein. What science fiction reader or gaming fan could resist such an opportunity? In my opinion, only those who were unaware of such a chance could pass it up! The only thing better could be more novels in the same setting combined with a role-playing game and the requisite scenarios . . . and that too will probably be available in time. Meanwhile, get ready for the fun and excitement offered herein.

This Chosen Path book allows you to adventure within the milieu of the universe of *Starship Troopers*, to actively participate in the story. You solve the problems, overcome the obstacles, direct the action, and arrive at the conclusion determined by your actions. Perhaps your first reading and play will result in the tragic demise of your character. Or, your initiation might bring your character to a non-heroic conclusion. No matter! Merely chalk it up to experience, take a deep breath, and start again. There are many wonderful features about a work such as this. One of the best is the long-term involvement possible. Unlike a regular novel, this one can be reread and replayed immediately, and often too. There are hours of adventure.

For the past decade or so I was too involved with the creation of fantasy materials to have the amount of involvement I desired with the genre of science fiction—my co-favorite since childhood. That has been changing recently. I've finally managed to write a short story for a series called "The Fleet," and some readers will have seen a science fiction role-playing game which I have co-created this year. In addition to the distinct honor of being able to introduce a work based on the writing of Robert Heinlein, it is also a great pleasure to be in a position to tell you that the book you have is a whole lot more than a novel—or even other multiple-choice, branching-path game books. This Chosen Path Combat Command Series book is one of outstanding merit and value. The imagination and imagery of Robert Heinlein brought to you for interactive participation is a science fiction fan's dream come true.

The adventure is awaiting, so get to it. There are aliens aplenty to defeat in the universe you are about to enter.

Gary Gygax
Lake Geneva, WI
1987

INTRODUCTION
by Bill Fawcett

You are in command. With a recorded blare of trumpets accented by a hurriedly barked order, it's off to battle. Entering the launch area behind you are men, trained warriors in their armored suits, whose lives depend upon the decisions you are about to make.

The Combat Command series puts you at the head of science fiction's toughest soldiers. In this book you command a squad of Robert Heinlein's Mobile Infantry (M.I.) on four of their most perilous missions. The Combat Command books provide one more chance to read about a well-known science fiction world and its familiar characters. These books are also a "game." In each section of this game book a military decision is described. You are given the same information you would actually receive in a real combat situation. At the end of each section is a number of choices. As the Mobile Infantry's commanding officer, you give the orders in battles against both the Bugs and the Skinnies. The consequences of your decision are described in the next section. When you make the right decisions, morale improves and you are closer to completing your mission. When you make a bad decision, men die . . . men who are not going to be available for future battles.

FIGHTING BATTLES

This book includes a simple game system that simulates combat and other military challenges. Playing the game adds an extra dimension of enjoyment by making you a participant in the adventure. You will need two six-sided dice, a pencil, and a sheet of paper to "play" along with this adventure.

COMBAT VALUES

Each unit is assigned five values. In a Combat Command book the force you command can consist of spaceships, armored infantry, mercenaries, or plasma- and laser-firing atomic tanks. These values provide the means of comparing the capabilities of the many different military units encountered in this book. These five values are:

Manpower

This value is the number of separate fighting parts of your force. Each unit of Manpower represents one man, one tank, or one spaceship. Casualties are subtracted from Manpower.

Ordnance

The quality and power of the weapons used by each M.I. trooper are reflected by their Ordnance value. All members of a unit commanded will have the same Ordnance value. In some cases you may command two or more units, each with a different Ordnance value.

Attack Strength

This value indicates the ability of the unit to attack an opponent. It is determined by multiplying Manpower by Ordnance (Manpower $\times$ Ordnance = Attack Strength).

This value can be different for every battle. It will decrease as Manpower is lost and increase if reinforcements are received.

Melee Strength

This is the hand-to-hand combat value of each member of the unit. In the case of a squad of mercenaries, it represents the martial-arts skill and training of each man. In crewed units such as tanks or spaceships, it represents the fighting ability of the members of the crew and could be used in an assault on a spaceport or to defend against boarders. Melee strength replaces the Ordnance value when determining the Attack Strength of a unit in hand-to-hand combat.

Stealth

This value measures how well the members of your unit can avoid detection. It represents the individual skill of each soldier or the ECM of each spaceship; in the case of the M.I., a bit of both. The Stealth value for your unit will be the same for each member of the unit. You would employ stealth to avoid detection by the enemy.

Morale

This reflects the fighting spirit of the troops you command. Success in battle may raise this value. Unpopular decisions or severe losses can lower it. If you order your unit to attempt something unusually dangerous, the outcome may be affected by their morale level. For example, in a situation where *you* are Teddy Roosevelt and have just ordered the Rough Riders to charge up San Juan Hill, the directions would read:

Roll two six-sided dice.
If the total rolled is the same as or less than the Rough Riders' Morale value, turn to section 24.

If the value rolled is greater than their current Morale value, turn to section 31.

In section 24, the Rough Riders follow you as Teddy Roosevelt up the hill and into history.

In section 31, they have lost faith in you and refuse to attack.

THE COMBAT PROCEDURE

When your squad of M.I. finds itself in a combat situation, use the following procedure to determine victory or defeat. This system uses a random dice roll combined with the situation itself to determine the casualties on both sides. You roll first for yourself and then for the enemy. The "hero" unit always fires first unless otherwise stated.

The steps to fight a combat are:

1. Compute the Attack Strength of your unit and the opposition, (Manpower × Ordnance or Melee Strength).

2. Turn to the charts at the end of this book that are given in the description of the battle. These will be used to determine each side's casualties.

3. Roll two six-sided dice and total the result.

4. Find the Attack Strength of the unit at the top of the chart and the total of the dice rolled on the left-hand column of the chart. The number found where the column and row intersect is the number of casualties inflicted.

5. Repeat for your opponent's side, alternating attacks until all of one side is eliminated.

When you are told there is a combat situation, you will be given all the information needed for both your command and their opponent. Also listed are any unusual factors and what effect they will have on the battle. All combat is resolved by a dice roll and the charts included at the end of this book.

Here is an example of a complete combat:

Hammer's Slammers have come under fire from a force defending a ridge that crosses their line of advance. Alois Hammer has ordered your company of tanks to attack.

Slammers fire using Chart B.

Locals fire using Chart D with an Ordnance value of 3 and Manpower of 12 (this will give them an Attack Strength of 36).

After three rounds of fire, the local force's morale breaks and the battle ends with their surrender.

To begin, you attack first and roll two 4s for a total of 8. The current Attack Strength of your Slammers is 64.

CHART B

Attack Strength

Dice Roll											
	1–10	–20	–30	–40	–50	–60	–70	–80	–90	–100	101+
2	0	0	0	1	1	1	2	2	2	3	4
3	0	0	1	1	1	2	2	2	3	3	4
4	0	1	1	1	2	2	2	3	3	3	4
5	1	1	1	2	2	2	3	3	3	4	5
6	1	1	2	2	2	3	3	3	4	4	5
7	1	2	2	2	3	3	3	4	4	4	5
8	2	2	2	3	3	3	4	4	4	5	6
9	2	2	3	3	3	4	4	4	5	5	6
10	2	3	3	3	4	4	4	5	5	5	6
11	3	3	3	4	4	4	5	5	5	6	7
12	3	3	4	4	4	5	5	6	6	7	8

Read down to the 60–70 Attack Strength column until you get to the line for a dice roll of 8. The result is 4 casualties inflicted on your opponents by your company.

Subtract these casualties from the opposing force before determining their Attack Strength. (Combat is not simultaneous.) After subtracting the 4 casualties you just inflicted on them, the enemy has a remaining Manpower value of 8 $(12 - 4 = 8)$. This gives them a remaining Attack Strength of 24 $(8 \times 3 = 24)$. Roll two six-sided dice for the opposing force's attack and determine the casualties they cause your Slammers' company. Subtract these casualties from your Manpower total on the record sheet. This ends one "round" of combat. Repeat the process for each round. Each time a unit receives a casualty, it will have a lower value for Attack Strength. There will be that many fewer men, tanks, spaceships, or whatever firing.

Continue alternating fire rolls, recalculating the Attack Strength each time to account for casualties, until one side or the other has lost all of its Manpower or special conditions (given in the text) apply. When this occurs, the battle is over. Losses are permanent and losses from your unit should be subtracted from their total manpower on the record sheet. You, the commander, are always the last casualty taken and so can be the sole survivor.

SNEAKING, HIDING, AND OTHER RECKLESS ACTS

To determine if a unit is successful in any attempt relating to Stealth or Morale, roll two six-sided dice. If the total rolled is greater than the value listed for the unit, the attempt fails. If the total of the two dice is the same as or less than the current value, the attempt succeeds or the action goes undetected. For example:

Rico decides his squad of Mobile Infantry (M.I.) will try to penetrate the Bug hole unseen. M.I. have a Stealth value of 8. A roll of 8 or less on two six-sided dice is needed to succeed. The dice are rolled and the result is a 4 and a 2 for a total of 6. They are able to avoid detection by the Bug guards.

If all of this is clear, then you are ready to turn to section 1 and take command. If you'd like another example of play, read on: You are in command of a ten-man U.S. Army patrol in France, World War II, fall 1944 . . . fade to the distant sound of artillery fire.

1st squad
2nd Platoon
B Company
2nd Battalion
29th Division
U.S. Army

Manpower 10

Ordnance 4

Stealth 9

Morale 10 (after all, we're winning)

Melee 5

This squad has an initial Attack Strength of 40 (4 × 10) in a firefight. It has an initial Attack Strength of 50 in a hand-to-hand melee (5 × 10).

Your squad is ordered to penetrate enemy lines to determine if a battery of artillery is concealed in the village of Soissons. There are no known German positions and the front is still fluid. You have crossed into Nazi-controlled territory and have been directed to turn to section 38.

— 38 —

You walked a long way since Omaha Beach and your feet were sore. As the squad moved through the last of the pickets you signaled for Corey Roberts to take the point. The trooper freed his M1 and trotted on ahead. The sun had just risen; the air was filled with the acrid odor of cordite from our own artillery. Somewhere, a few miles in the rear, you could hear the roar of a battery firing on some unseen target. Everyone hoped it would distract the Nazis, but knew better.

The next few hundred yards were uneventful. The front was new here. Neither side had had time to establish a continuous line. Suddenly Lewis whispered an urgent command and everyone froze. Up ahead Roberts was crouched behind a tree and gestured at a clump of bushes a few yards ahead of him.

After a few tense moments you could see the first German as he emerged from the bushes. Moments later three more followed. All were armed with submachine guns and wore the black uniforms of the SS. They were moving very cautiously. The Germans didn't appear to have spotted you.

If you attack the German patrol, turn to section 41.

If you try to remain concealed and let them pass, turn to section 42.

— 41 —

The Americans attack on Chart B.

The Germans fire back on Chart D. Their submachine guns have a firepower of 6, giving them an initial Attack Strength of 24.

If you win the battle, turn to section 55.

If you are defeated, turn to section 29.

The American patrol attacks first. You roll two six-sided dice and total them. They are a 4 and 3 for a total of 7. Looking down the column for an Attack Strength of 40 until you reach the row for a dice roll of 7, we see you killed 2 of the Nazis.

The reader would then roll for the 2 remaining Germans' return fire. In this case he rolls a 4 and a 5 for a total of 9. Since each German with an SMG has an Ordnance value of 6, this gives the two men a remaining Attack Strength of 12 (2 × 6). Looking in the 1–20 column of Chart D next to the 9, we see they cause 1 casualty. One man is subtracted from the Manpower of the American patrol, leaving a total now of 9 men and an Attack Strength of 36 (9 × 4 = 36, as the Ordnance value of the remaining men never changes).

This completes one round of combat.

A second round is then begun with the Americans again firing first. Two six-sided dice are rolled for a total of 10. Checking on Chart B in the 30–40 column for a roll of 10, we find that this fire was sufficient to kill 3 more Nazis. As only 2 remained, the combat is over immediately (there being no return fire from the SS troopers as they are all dead). The combat is over and you would turn to section 55.

— 42 —

Roll two six-sided dice. If the total is 9 or less, turn to
section 46.

If the total is greater than 9, turn to section 47.

Here you are trying to remain undetected and so will be
rolling against the squad's Stealth value, which is 9. Any
total except a 10, 11, or 12 would indicate success. If the
two dice were to roll a 5 and a 2 for a total of 7, your
patrol will escape detection. You would then turn to section 46 and continue the mission.

It is now time for you to assume command of your own
squad of Mobile Infantry. Good luck, trooper.

Turn to section 1.

THE COMBAT CHARTS

After you have made a decision involving a battle, you will be told which chart should be used for your unit and which for the enemy. The chart used is determined by the tactical and strategic situation. Chart A is used when the unit is most effective and Chart G when least effective. Chart A represents the effectiveness of the Sioux at Little Bighorn and Chart F, Custer. Chart G represents the equivalent of classic Zulus with aseiges (spears) versus modern Leopard tanks. Even a very small force on Chart A can be effective, while even a large number of combatants attacking on Chart G are unlikely to have much effect.

CHART A

Dice Roll	1–10	–20	–30	–40	–50	–60	–70	–80	–90	–100	101+
2	0	1	1	2	2	3	3	4	5	6	6
3	0	1	2	2	2	3	4	5	6	7	7
4	1	2	2	2	3	3	4	5	6	7	8
5	2	2	2	3	3	4	5	5	6	7	8
6	2	2	2	3	4	4	5	6	7	7	8
7	2	2	3	4	4	5	5	6	7	8	8
8	2	3	3	4	4	5	6	6	7	8	9
9	3	3	4	4	5	5	6	7	8	8	9
10	3	4	4	5	5	6	7	7	8	9	10
11	3	4	4	5	6	6	7	8	9	10	11
12	4	4	5	6	7	7	8	9	10	11	12

CHART B

Dice Roll	1–10	–20	–30	–40	–50	–60	–70	–80	–90	–100	101+
2	0	0	0	1	1	1	2	2	2	3	4
3	0	0	1	1	1	2	2	2	3	3	4
4	0	1	1	1	2	2	2	3	3	3	4
5	1	1	1	2	2	2	3	3	3	4	5
6	1	1	2	2	2	3	3	3	4	4	5
7	1	2	2	2	3	3	3	4	4	4	5
8	2	2	2	3	3	3	4	4	4	5	6
9	2	2	3	3	3	4	4	4	5	5	6
10	2	3	3	3	4	4	4	5	5	5	6
11	3	3	3	4	4	4	5	5	5	6	7
12	3	3	4	4	4	5	5	6	6	7	8

CHART C

Dice Roll	1–10	–20	–30	–40	–50	–60	–70	–80	–90	–100	101+
2	0	0	0	0	0	1	1	1	2	2	2
3	0	0	0	0	1	1	1	2	2	2	3
4	0	0	0	1	1	1	2	2	2	3	3
5	0	0	1	1	1	2	2	2	3	3	4
6	0	1	1	1	2	2	2	3	3	3	4
7	1	1	1	2	2	2	3	3	3	4	5
8	1	1	2	2	2	3	3	3	4	4	5
9	1	2	2	2	3	3	3	4	4	5	5
10	2	2	2	3	3	3	4	4	4	5	6
11	2	2	3	3	3	4	4	4	5	5	6
12	2	3	3	3	4	4	4	5	5	6	7

CHART D

Dice Roll	1–10	–20	–30	–40	–50	–60	–70	–80	–90	–100	101+
2	0	0	0	0	0	0	0	1	1	1	2
3	0	0	0	0	0	0	1	1	1	2	2
4	0	0	0	0	0	1	1	1	2	2	2
5	0	0	0	0	1	1	1	2	2	2	3
6	0	0	0	1	1	1	2	2	2	3	3
7	0	0	1	1	1	2	2	2	3	3	4
8	0	1	1	1	2	2	2	3	3	4	4
9	1	1	1	2	2	2	3	3	3	4	5
10	1	1	2	2	2	3	3	3	4	4	5
11	1	2	2	2	3	3	3	4	4	5	5
12	2	2	2	3	3	3	4	4	5	5	6

CHART E

Dice Roll	1–10	–20	–30	–40	–50	–60	–70	–80	–90	–100	101+
2	0	0	0	0	0	0	0	0	0	1	1
3	0	0	0	0	0	0	0	0	1	1	1
4	0	0	0	0	0	0	0	1	1	1	2
5	0	0	0	0	0	0	1	1	1	2	2
6	0	0	0	0	0	1	1	1	1	2	2
7	0	0	0	0	1	1	1	1	2	2	2
8	0	0	0	1	1	1	1	2	2	2	2
9	0	0	1	1	1	1	2	2	2	2	2
10	0	1	1	1	1	2	2	2	2	2	3
11	1	1	1	1	2	2	2	2	2	3	3
12	1	1	1	2	2	2	2	2	2	3	3

CHART F

Dice Roll	1–10	–20	–30	–40	–50	–60	–70	–80	–90	–100	101+
2	0	0	0	0	0	0	0	0	0	0	0
3	0	0	0	0	0	0	0	0	0	0	0
4	0	0	0	0	0	0	0	0	0	0	0
5	0	0	0	0	0	0	0	0	0	0	0
6	0	0	0	0	0	0	0	0	0	0	1
7	0	0	0	0	0	0	0	0	0	0	1
8	0	0	0	0	0	0	0	0	0	1	1
9	0	0	0	0	0	0	0	0	1	1	1
10	0	0	0	0	0	0	0	1	1	1	1
11	1	1	1	1	1	1	1	1	1	1	2
12	1	1	1	1	1	1	1	1	1	2	3

CHART G

Dice Roll	1–10	–20	–30	–40	–50	–60	–70	–80	–90	–100	101+
2	0	0	0	0	0	0	0	0	0	0	0
3	0	0	0	0	0	0	0	0	0	0	0
4	0	0	0	0	0	0	0	0	0	0	0
5	0	0	0	0	0	0	0	0	0	0	0
6	0	0	0	0	0	0	0	0	0	0	0
7	0	0	0	0	0	0	0	0	0	0	0
8	0	0	0	0	0	0	0	0	0	0	0
9	0	0	0	0	0	0	0	0	0	0	0
10	0	0	0	0	0	0	0	0	0	0	1
11	0	0	0	0	0	0	0	0	0	1	1
12	1	1	1	1	1	1	1	1	1	1	1

STANDARD TROOP VALUES
STARSHIP TROOPERS

All Mobile Infantry (M.I.) have the following values unless otherwise specified:

Ordnance: 7   Melee: 5   Morale: 9

All Bug warriors have the following values unless otherwise specified:

Ordnance: 3   Melee: 4   Morale: N/A

All Skinny troops have the following values unless otherwise specified:

Ordnance: 3   Melee: 3   Morale: Varies 2–5

The low Skinny morale means they will often break off a firefight after just a few rounds of combat.

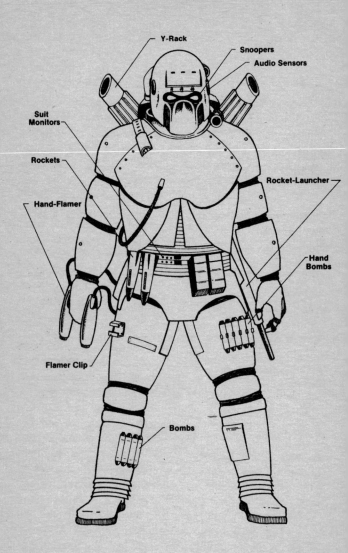

Y-Rack

Snoopers

Audio Sensors

Suit
Monitors

Rockets

Hand-Flamer

Rocket-Launcher

Hand
Bombs

Flamer Clip

Bombs

—1—

"Paolo! Head for the beacon. On the bounce!"

Julian snapped the command, jumped, loaded his rocket launcher, shut off the helmet tactical display, and took a visual sighting with his infrared snooper. His finger squeezed the launcher trigger twice. The rocket leapt toward its target as Julian hit the top of his bounce.

That takes care of the Bug reserves headed Paolo's way, Julian thought. In five seconds, they'll be just so much radioactive dust, caught up in a two-kiloton fireball. Blast Paolo, anyway. He knows better than to lag behind, especially on an emergency hit-and-run drop. Discipline . . . discipline is the key to any successful military operation. Discipline is what Paolo lacks, and discipline is what Paolo will have to get. But there'll be plenty of time to take care of that once we're off Birgu and back aboard the good ship *Colonel Bowie*.

Plenty to worry about without Paolo. This drop has been a fiasco from the beginning. Next item: be sure Brennan has the special talent headed toward the beacon. Julian switched back to tactical display and heaved a sigh of relief as his helmet radar showed Brennan less than one mile from the retrieval point. He reloaded the rocket launcher with his last atomic, fired, and hit the ground in one motion, rolling to avoid the shock wave from his two-kiloton present to the Bugs. As soon as the wave passed over, he took another bounce, visually scanning for any local opposition.

Five seconds gone, and still no answer from Paolo!

The last thought knocked all others from Julian's mind. He was at the top of his bounce, and had visual sighting of Wade and Sutu in full retreat toward the retrieval point. He was just beginning to feel that the squad might make it through this disaster when surprise turned to rage at Paolo's insubordination.

"Paolo! Answer me now, soldier!" Julian barked.

"Julian! Roll! Incoming!"

Wade's voice was a half-second too late. The shock from the bomb caught Julian halfway down, and he tumbled out of control to the ground.

"Squad leader down! Sutu—you have the bearing?"

"I've got it. Make the pickup. I'm laying down flamer cover."

Julian rolled face-up in time to see Sutu's flamer incinerate two Bugs less than fifteen yards from his own sprawled body. Wade was already bounding toward him, the HE bombs pouring from the Y-rack on his back in a dangerously tight pattern.

"Julian, I'm coming for pickup. Stay steady!"

By the time Wade's words registered, Julian had realized the situation. In his surprise and anger at Paolo, he had jumped into the middle of a Bug counterattack. Bug warriors were boiling out of the ground all around him, and he'd been so angry, he hadn't even noticed. The blast that had knocked him down had been a bomb launched by the alert Wade into the Bug mass. The explosion that downed him had saved his life.

"Wade, back out. I'm okay. Sutu, cover Wade out of this mess. Both of you, head for the retrieval point. Boat lands in seventy-five seconds. Remember, getting Brennan's special talent on board has top priority. I'm going after Paolo. And, Wade . . . thanks."

Julian was in the air again in four seconds. During those seconds he learned to be thankful for the efficiency of powered armor and the wonderful area effects of the hand flamer. Above all, he was grateful for the tenacious, bulldog stubbornness of boot camp instructor Sergeant Zim, who had literally beaten the manly art of hand-to-hand combat into the very synapses of Julian's central nervous system. Yes, indeed, Julian thought as he dropped a hand bomb down the last Bug hole, every bruise was worth it.

Now to find Paolo. He still hadn't answered verbally, and didn't show on the radar tactical display. Great. Another situation not covered by the book. Julian bounced toward Paolo's last radar fix, covering the flat, dusty ground at ten yards per second and feeling every precious one of those seconds slipping away.

Every man in the Mobile Infantry knows that, in combat, seconds are the most precious things in the universe. In the words of Captain John Rico, ". . . seconds are jewels beyond price in combat. While off the ground in a jump, you can get a range and bearing, pick a target, talk and receive, fire a weapon, reload, decide to jump again without landing, and override your automatics to cut in the jets again. You can do all of these things in one bounce, with practice." Julian had had plenty of practice.

What Rico didn't mention is that every single M.I. had better make the best possible use of every one of those seconds, because there comes a point in every M.I. hit-and-run operation when time is on the enemy's side. While the M.I. are bouncing around in powered armor, sowing havoc and destruction, the enemy's defenses are responding: locating the M.I., assessing their strength and probable objective, deploying stronger forces to intercept and destroy the raiders. It isn't enough for the M.I. to get in undetected and hit their objective. They have to get in and hit that objective *fast*. Every second after contact with the enemy, their chances of getting out again go down.

That's not all. The situation is worse when the enemy is the Bugs, an intelligent cross between insect and arachnid. Bugs don't live on the ground; they live under it, deep under it in extensive tunnel mazes. When they take over a planet, the surviving native population stays on the surface as a captive labor force and potential target for Terran Federation attacks, while the Bug overlords and occupying forces are secure deep underground. There aren't many ways for a raiding force to know where the Bugs are located, where their tunnels run, where their strength lies. Worse, the Bugs can make new tunnels with amazing speed. A few minutes after the M.I. hit the ground, their drop zone can be swarming with Bug warriors boiling out of new holes on the planet's surface.

Bug warriors are implacable foes. They don't know pain, they don't know fear, they never break and run. At least, from a soldier's perspective these are the facts. The scientists on Terra may learn more about the Bugs someday. Maybe the ugly black things do have feelings, but as far as a soldier is concerned, they might as well be robots. A Bug warrior can be burned, blown in half, or beaten to a squished pulp. The thing'll keep coming, even if it's the last one left of its unit. It absolutely will not quit. It was born and bred for only one purpose, to kill M.I. or die trying.

The brain-caste Bugs are a separate type altogether. They stay deep below the surface and direct operations. No one knows how they communicate with the warriors, but this type of hive animal division of labor makes it almost impossible to disrupt a Bug chain of command. The only way to do it is to go underground, root out the brains. Dangerous work. So far, no one has written the book on how to do it; no one who's gone down a Bug hole has lived long enough.

A human chain of command, on the other hand, can be disrupted easily. In theory, there's always the next man down the line, ready to take over if the man giving the orders buys the farm. Sometimes it works that way. But given human nature, no matter how intensively trained, sometimes it doesn't. Unlike Bugs, humans can panic, rout, or become gripped by fear. They can let fear drive them to take the absolutely worst possible course of action in a combat situation.

Maybe that's what happened to Paolo, Julian mused as he closed on that last radar fix. Worse yet, here's my squad, less than sixty seconds left to retrieval, and the

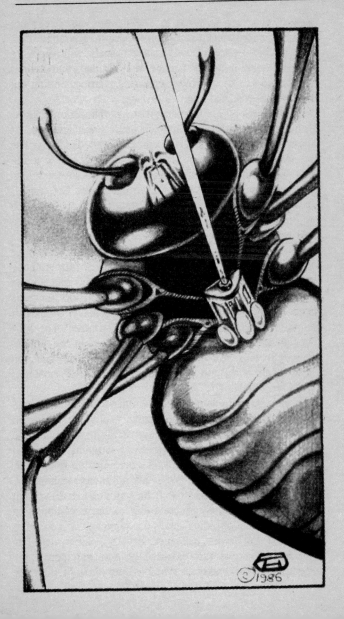

©1986

squad leader is out bounding around headed heaven knows where because discipline has already started to break down. There goes the chain of command!

Not enough that my first time out as a squad commander had to be a special emergency drop. Not enough the battalion's drop was spotted by the Bug sensors right away. Nothing like sitting helpless in your drop capsule while the atmosphere burns away its skins like layers of an onion, and Bug missiles are homing in with deadly accuracy. Not enough that our squad was the only one to land without casualties, and so pulled the big mission assignment, retrieval of a special missions agent who had to get off this piece of rock before he became Bug bait. Nope. I had to get Paolo, too.

At least the mission is going to be successful, assuming the survivors make the retrieval boat, assuming the retrieval boat doesn't get blasted on the way to the mother ship, and assuming the good old *Colonel Bowie* gets away without being atomized. Hope it's worth it, all for one special talent. Seems like a lot of trouble to retrieve one man from a Bug-infested planet, even if he can sense out Bug tunnels from the surface and map them in his mind. Julian hoped the special talent's mind was still intact as Brennan carried the non-armored man to the retrieval point.

"Paolo, report. That's a direct order!"

Julian practically shouted the command. His frustration was reaching the boiling point again.

"Hey man, stay loose." It was Paolo's voice. "I'm down a Bug hole, lookin' around, man. Everything's okay."

"Guiterez, you ape! On the bounce! Get up here and report to the retrieval point. We've just got time to make it."

"Sure, on my way. Really, man, you got to watch that temper. Losing emotional control in a combat situation makes you look, you know, unfit for command of a squad, don't you think?"

So that's Paolo's game. How had this idiot gotten through boot camp? It is inconceivable that a trained M.I. in a combat situation would jeopardize his entire unit to pursue a personal vendetta, but that's exactly what this looks like, Julian thought. Would Paolo really endanger the entire battalion over Brenda?

Sure he would. Julian answered his own question with a sinking sigh. He suddenly felt tired, very tired. He could remember the day Brenda first walked into his classroom and into a prominent role in his life. He had been seventeen years old, a naive kid then, full of himself. Paolo had been just as cocksure, and filled with *machissmo*. Could he help it if Brenda preferred him? In a war, though, it is not unheard of for soldiers on the same side to fight personal battles as fierce—and as deadly—as those against the enemy.

Paolo's highly insubordinate remarks were broadcast on the general circuit—every member of Julian's squad had heard what Paolo said. Wade, Sutu, and Brennan seemed to be good men. They had respected authority, so far, whether or not they respected the man who had temporary custody of that authority. But they'd be listening now, for sure, to hear how Julian would handle this direct challenge from Paolo.

"The thinking, soldier, is my job. Your job is following orders. Now, move it!"

Julian tried to sound as stern as he could without sounding like a screaming maniac, totally out of control. He waited only long enough to see Paolo emerge from the Bug hole, then bounced back toward the retrieval point. Paolo followed.

"Penn! Forty-five seconds! Report!"

Sergeant Stakowski's voice crackled over the section leader's command circuit. Stakowski was very big, very tough, very much "on the bounce, by the book." He had personally recommended Julian for his corporal's stripe and carefully trained him in the duties of a squad leader. Now he wanted to know where his handpicked squad leader happened to be. He also wanted to know a few other things like why, in the middle of a combat situation, the squad leader wasn't with his squad, which had the most important assignment of the entire mission. Julian switched to his private circuit to Sergeant Stakowski.

"Brennan is carrying the special talent to the retrieval beacon. Privates Wade and Sutu closing on beacon. They may have company and might require covering fire from the retrieval shield."

"Right. I have all three on visual. Retrieval boats also on visual. Now, mister, state your position!"

Stakowski already knew Julian's position. Both men knew Stakowski could see Julian on his command radar display. Obviously, Julian thought, the sarge wants me to be aware of my position, in more ways than one. But why did he say "boats"? There should be only one.

"Bearing from beacon three-one-five, range zero point six and closing on the bounce, Sarge."

"That's just great, son. Bugs boiling for counterattack three hundred yards dead ahead of you. Rest of the section is cut off out of position, being retrieved by a boat from the *Alvin York*. I know, it's a change of plan. We're improvising here. Wade, Sutu, and Brennan can make the boat from the *Colonel Bowie*. There'll be no covering fire from the shield—you might have guessed that by now. Try to get past the Bugs as best you can. Once Brennan has the special talent on the boat, the order is *sauve qui peut*. Do you understand?"

"Right, Sarge. Get Brennan on the boat, then *sauve qui peut*. Good luck, Sarge."

"Shine, soldier."

It was bad, very bad. Julian's squad had been the right flank of the section, which was the right flank of the entire battalion. If the section was cut off from the *Colonel Bowie* boat, that meant the battalion was disintegrating. No soldier needed to know what *sauve qui peut* meant. It was the order every M.I. hoped he'd never hear: Every man for himself.

Julian saw the Bugs from the top of his next bounce. He checked his tactical display: Brennan was at the retrieval point, the boat was coming down. Wade and Sutu were standing still, about a hundred yards from the retrieval point. He clicked to his squad circuit.

"Brennan. Board the boat immediately with your package. Wade, Sutu, cover Brennan and board right after him. Paolo, Bugs at twelve o'clock. Alternate bounces, fire hand flamers from ground position and top of the bounce. If you make it past them, set the Y-rack on automatic and make for the boat. *Sauve qui peut.* I'm on the ground, you bounce first. By the numbers. One!"

Julian's hand flamer spat death at the nearest Bug while he silently counted to himself. Bugs were boiling out of the ground like locusts. With three hundred yards more to cover to the retrieval boat, there was almost no chance of making it. Paolo sailed past overhead, firing a wide flamer pattern from the top of his bounce. At least he was following orders.

"Two!"

Julian jumped, checking his tactical display again and picking a target on the way up. Brennan will make the boat! At least we'll die for something. Julian fired. A Bug flared.

"Three!"

Julian hit the ground and fired again. A flaming Bug dropped three feet in front of him, its legs burned off, its mandibles still clicking. Tactical display showed Brennan aboard the boat. What were Wade and Sutu waiting for?

"Four!"

Bounce. Fire. Lean out of the Bug line of fire. Set the Y-rack, no, wait; Paolo's behind me. Let him get clear first on his next bounce.

"Five!"

The ground in front of Julian erupted. A snap of his head brought down the infrared snoopers, the only way to see through the dust from the explosion. He saw Paolo fall from a height of ten feet and land flat on his back. He wasn't moving. Amazing—Julian had no idea the Bugs could lay mines that fast—or had it just been a lucky bomb? Anyway, Paolo was down.

"Six!"

Julian called the number and jumped from pure reflex. He sailed over Paolo's motionless form in the small crater where he had landed.

"Boat ready for launch! Julian! Paolo! Ready to launch!"

Wade's news was hardly welcome. A retrieval boat has a very, very tight launch window. If it misses by more than a few seconds, odds are very good it will miss rendezvous with the mother ship. A mother ship pilot over Bug-occupied worlds has bigger things to worry about than picking up a retrieval boat. One false move and the ship is dust.

"Julian! Come on! Paolo, on the bounce. This baby's got to go!"

"Paolo! Answer!" Julian cried from the top of his bounce. His flamer incinerated one of the half-dozen Bugs already swarming toward the body. Another half-dozen Bugs were in sight, firing at Julian.

No answer from Paolo.

The sarge's orders were clear. *Sauve qui peut*. Every man for himself. At the same time, Julian knew that there is one very old, very respected M.I. tradition: the M.I. take care of their own. Paolo might be dead, but he might be only wounded, unconscious, unable to respond.

If Julian leaves Paolo and heads to the retrieval boat, go to section 3.

If Julian tries to save Paolo single-handedly, go to section 4.

If Julian orders Wade and Sutu to assist him in picking up Paolo, go to section 2.

— 2 —

"Wade, Sutu. Paolo's down. Bearing three-one-five, range zero point one-one. Bugs everywhere. I make twelve on visual in immediate range. Belay boat launch. Close and lay down fire to assist pickup. On the bounce! Brennan, sit tight and guard the goods. Launch in forty-five seconds."

The M.I. take care of their own. Julian made his decision and snapped his orders before he hit the ground again, spinning to reverse direction at the start of his next bounce. Maybe it is every man for himself, Julian thought, but I won't leave Paolo behind to become Bug bait, even if this foul-up is his own stupid fault.

In the air, Julian fired his flamer and set his Y-rack for tight pattern automatic. The HE bombs began scattering to his left and right, behind him. The pattern should still leave room for Wade and Sutu to close. Tactical display showed them coming, advancing by the numbers, just like in a tactical combat drill.

There are twelve Bugs in the battle. Use Chart E for their attack.

Julian fires using Chart D.

Julian fights two rounds alone. If he is still unhurt after two rounds of battle, Wade and Sutu arrive, increasing the number of M.I. to three. The Bugs fight for only two rounds after Wade and Sutu arrive, then scatter down their holes.

If Julian takes any hits before Wade and Sutu arrive, go to section 6.

If the M.I. win the fight with no casualties, go to section 5.

If the M.I. win the fight but suffer one casualty, go to section 7.

If the M.I. win the fight but suffer two casualties, go to section 8.

If the Bugs win the fight, go to section 29.

— 3 —

Tradition or no, Julian decided, Paolo messed up. It's his own fault he's lying in a Bug bomb crater. It's not worth risking the whole squad, not to mention the whole mission that so many men have already died for, just to pull him out.

"I'm coming in. Paolo's done for," Julian radioed.

A few more bounces brought Julian to the boarding ramp of the retrieval boat. HE bombs, fired automatically from the Y-rack on his back, kept the Bugs at bay.

"Boat away!" Julian ordered, clambering up the ramp. The ramp swung up and Julian dived for a couch. The g-force of acceleration pushed him face-down into the warm cot. The pressure was terrible, but the cot felt good nonetheless. It was warm, it was secure, it was safe.

The retrieval boat pilot worked a few small wonders, and so did the pilot of the *Colonel Bowie*. Within twenty minutes, Julian's squad was safely aboard the mother ship. Technicians helped check out and stow the armored suits. Julian, Wade, Sutu, and Brennan had the M.I. quarters of the ship to themselves; the remaining survivors of the battalion were aboard the *Alvin York*.

Silence ruled in those quarters. Julian noticed that the unloading duties were accompanied by none of the usual banter that was bandied about after a drop. At first, he thought there was nothing wrong with this. It had been a hard drop; the men were tired. He saw to the unloading and reported to the ship's captain, summarizing what he knew of the operation on the ground.

The captain filled Julian in on the overall situation. Apparently, the Bugs were expecting company. They must have spotted the special talent some time ago, because they were lying in wait to ambush his retrieval force. Thanks to Julian's squad, the special talent had gotten away safely. In fact, he was in another part of the ship right now, being debriefed by a special mission team composed of very hush-hush, tight-lipped intelligence types. The *Colonel Bowie* had taken several direct hits during the drop, and only one of her retrieval boats was functional. That's why the remainder of the battalion had been retrieved in boats from the *Alvin York*.

Overall, casualties had been heavy. Ten percent of the men were hit in their capsules on the way down. Somehow, the Bug missile-guidance system had gotten lucky against all the radar chaff those capsules threw off in descent. The captain could only spare five minutes' time to brief Julian; she had a ship to run. But before she dismissed him, the captain handed Julian a subspace message:

FROM: Third Lt. Abram Weiss
TO: Corporal Julian Penn
RE: Immediate Orders

Be advised I am now acting commander of Second Platoon, Company E, First Battalion, Second Regiment, First Mobile Infantry Division.

Upon arrival Sanctuary, take temporary command of second section of platoon with brevet rank of sergeant and await further orders.

Good work.

Julian's elation was gone when he finished reading the message. His breveting to section command could mean only one thing: both Sergeant Stakowski and the assistant section leader had bought the farm.

Julian went aft, fighting back tears of anger and sorrow. Stakowski had been a good man, a good friend, even if he was a sergeant. The news would certainly demoralize the squad. Even worse, a third lieutenant was in temporary command of the platoon. That meant the entire higher chain of command had gone down, given the supreme sacrifice.

When Julian arrived in the bunk room, the silence from his squad was still total. Worse, no one would look him in the eyes.

"All right," Julian began, "it was a rough one, but we got the job done. Brennan, good work."

"Thank you, Corporal Penn." Brennan lay down and rolled over, turning his back to Julian.

"Wade, Sutu, thanks for your help when that Bug wave boiled up."

Wade nodded without speaking, then looked away.

"Certainly, Corporal. It is my understanding that the M.I. take care of their own," Sutu said softly. The big black man sat on the edge of his bunk, his eyes riveted on the floor. Slowly, he turned to meet Julian's gaze directly. "I intend to continue acting on that understanding."

"Meaning exactly what, Private Sutu?"

"Meaning this, Corporal Penn. I will obey your lawful orders. Next time you're down I'll try to help you out, make a pickup, even though, in my personal opinion, you as an individual do not deserve such help. In short, corporal, you needn't worry about my doing my duty. I will do my duty despite the fact that you, my immediate superior, cannot be relied upon to help a wounded comrade."

Private Matsusu Sutu chose his words carefully. Sutu was a careful, deliberate, serious man. Speaking in front of witnesses, he would say nothing that directly challenged or rejected Julian's authority. But Julian had asked what he meant, and he left no doubt as to his meaning.

"In short, Corporal Penn, I'll do my duty, but I won't trust you any farther than I can spit."

Brennan rolled over, Wade looked up. Sutu challenged Julian's gaze.

"I take it," Julian said slowly, "this has to do with my command decision not to make pickup on Paolo."

"Command decision my boot!" Brennan shouted. The florid-faced soldier leapt to his feet. "You left one of our squad for the Bugs because you were too lily-livered to make pickup. We could have helped—we would have helped. But you just left him—you didn't even bother to check his vital signs."

"Are you accusing me of cowardice in combat?" Julian regretted the question the minute it left his lips. When would he learn to control his temper? Brennan was as hotheaded as Julian, and if he answered yes to that question with witnesses present, it would mean a court-martial for one of them, perhaps both.

Brennan stared hard at Julian for what seemed like an eternity. Sutu broke the silence.

"I believe Private Brennan misspoke himself, Corporal Penn. I do not believe Private Brennan wishes to make a formal accusation at this time."

"Yeah. That's right. I do not wish to make a formal accusation of cowardice in combat . . . at this time. Cowardice in combat is a capital offense," Brennan said. The burly man spoke very slowly, measuring his words through his anger. "I don't want to see you killed, Penn, because there may be something about you I don't know, something that would make it worthwhile to have you alive. You have any suggestions?"

Brennan's challenge was clear enough, Julian thought. He thinks I'm a coward, but he's not absolutely certain and he doesn't want to press a general court-martial. Either I dispel that impression now, or I have a squad whose obedience depends solely on regulations, not on any positive feelings of comradeship.

If Julian decides to invite Brennan down to the ship's gym to "put on the gloves," go to section 10.

If Julian decides not to challenge Brennan, go to section 11.

Regardless of Julian's decision, lower the squad's Morale by 1 as the result of Julian's leaving Paolo behind.

— 4 —

"Wade, Sutu. Paolo's down. Bearing three-one-five, range zero point one-one. Bugs everywhere. I make twelve on visual in immediate range. Try to hold the boat! Brennan, sit tight and guard the goods. Launch without delay if I'm not back in forty-five seconds."

The M.I. take care of their own. Julian made his decision and snapped his orders before he hit the ground again, spinning to reverse direction at the start of his next bounce. Maybe it is every man for himself, Julian thought, but I won't leave Paolo behind to become Bug bait, even if this foul-up is his own stupid fault.

In the air, Julian fired his flamer and set his Y-rack for tight pattern automatic. The HE bombs began scattering to his left and right, behind him, blowing oncoming Bugs to bits.

There are twelve Bugs in the battle. Use Chart E for their attack.

Julian fires using Chart D.

Julian fights two rounds alone. If he is still unhurt after two rounds of battle, the Bugs scatter down their holes.

If Julian takes any hit, go to section 6.

If Julian takes no hits in the two rounds of combat, go to section 9.

— 5 —

Hot flaming space! With a squad like this, a guy could lick the whole Bug army, given half a chance.

Julian suppressed these exuberant thoughts as his squad made for the retrieval-boat ramp. Sutu, the tall, strong black man from central Africa, was laughing out loud at Paolo, who was complaining to Wade in his finest Latino style.

"Hey man, take it easy! You took my armor off, remember? I'm not padded all around like you. My head is throbbing. You trying to kill me with the headache, man? Take it easy on these bounces!"

Paolo had been very, very lucky. He'd landed point-blank on a Bug mine, but lived to tell about it. His armor was in tatters, but the crazy Latin had taken nothing worse than a bump on the head and a few superficial cuts. Apparently his jets had kicked in at the same time the mine went off. Lucky indeed.

Sutu and Wade had shown up on the bounce and fought like demons. After a taste of their flamers and HE bombs, the Bug brain had apparently thought better of this little skirmish. The Bug warriors scurried down their holes. Wade stripped Paolo out of his armor while Julian and Sutu dropped bombs down the holes after the Bugs.

"Board retrieval boat!" Julian sang out happily. He was

the last one up the ramp. He threw himself onto a launch cot as the boat's thrusters kicked in. Somehow, the boat pilot and the mother ship pilot managed to work a couple of miracles between them, and within twenty minutes Julian's men were exchanging the usual post-action banter aboard the *Colonel Bowie*.

Julian reported forward to the ship's captain and got the word on the operation. Apparently, the Bugs were expecting company. They must have spotted the special talent some time ago, because they were lying in wait to ambush his retrieval force. Thanks to Julian's squad, the special talent had gotten away safely. In fact, he was in another part of the ship right now, being debriefed by a special mission team composed of very hush-hush, tight-lipped intelligence types. The squad would have the M.I quarters on the *Colonel Bowie* to themselves for the voyage back to Fleet Base on Sanctuary. The rest of the battalions were jammed aboard the *Alvin York*. The *Colonel Bowie* had taken several direct hits during the drop, and only one of her boats had been functional to make retrieval.

Overall, casualties had been heavy. Ten percent of the men were hit in their capsules on the way down. Somehow, the Bug missile-guidance system had gotten lucky against all the radar chaff those capsules threw off in descent. The captain could only spare five minutes' time to brief Julian; she had a ship to run. But before she dismissed him, the captain handed Julian a subspace message:

FROM: Third Lt. Abram Weiss
TO: Corporal Julian Penn
RE: Immediate Orders

Be advised I am now acting commander of Second Platoon, Company E, First Battalion, Second Regiment, First Mobile Infantry Division.

Upon arrival Sanctuary, take temporary command of second

section of platoon with brevet rank of sergeant and await further orders.

Good work.

Julian's elation was gone when he finished reading the message. His breveting to section command could mean only one thing: both Sergeant Stakowski and the assistant section leader had bought the farm.

Julian went aft, fighting back tears of anger and sorrow. Stakowski had been a good man, a good friend, even if he was a sergeant. The news would certainly demoralize the squad. Even worse, a third lieutenant was in temporary command of the platoon. That meant the entire higher chain of command had gone down, given the supreme sacrifice.

As he rounded the corner to M.I. quarters, a voice stopped Julian in his tracks. It was Sutu's voice, drifting down the corridor.

"Yes. I'm sure you were doing everything by the book, Paolo. That's why Penn had to go off looking for you." Sutu, as always, was calm and deliberate, choosing his words with care. "You are quite fortunate your wounds were superficial and that we weren't all killed trying to rescue you from your own folly."

"That's right, you crazy Latin!" Brennan joined in. The big, burly Brennan was seldom as careful as Sutu about what he said. Brennan had a temper, and even M.I. training hadn't yet taught him to master it. "You almost got us all killed, and for nothing! So you could stick your nose in a Bug hole!"

"Oh yeah, man? Well, you stow it, man," Paolo shouted back in his best self-righteous tone. "When the Bugs wipe out your hometown, you come tell me how it feels. You come tell me how you're not going to stick your nose down every Bug hole you can until those black horrors are dead meat. By the book, my boot! Penn can speak for himself. If he isn't man enough to chew me out himself, you won't do any good trying to do it for him. Besides, the man was out of control. If he'd been on the bounce, we'd have made it back fine in plenty of time.''

Paolo turned to see what Brennan, Sutu, and Wade were staring at. His eyes met Julian's.

''Yeah, so, I say the same thing to your face, man,'' Paolo barked, toughing it out.

I have three real options, Julian thought. Oh, I can do what I want to do more than anything in the world: thrash this ungrateful jerk here and now, in front of the whole squad. But that's not an option for a squad commander. I can thrash him in private; that's the M.I. tradition. Or I can call for a general court-martial. Doesn't this fool know that disobeying orders in combat is a capital offense? If I say the word, he'll be dancing Danny Deever at the end of a rope before we've spent twelve hours in Sanctuary. Or, I can do nothing.

If Julian decides to thrash Paolo in private, go to section 13.

If Julian decides to bring Paolo up before a court-martial, go to section 14.

If Julian decides to ignore Paolo's behavior, go to section 12.

— 6 —

Pain. Pain, like a thousand hot knitting needles rammed through his skull. Pain was the first thing, and for a while the only thing, Julian felt.

Gradually, with great effort, he forced open his eyes.

"Unnnh . . ." was the best he could manage to say.

"Ah, waking up at last, you lazy soldier?"

The room slowly came into focus. Julian saw that the speaker was a ship's surgeon assistant. Had he been in a normal condition, he might have noticed she was an attractive one, but such thoughts were beyond his current capability.

"I know, I know. A hundred questions." She smiled as she checked the tubes attached to his body. "You M.I. boys are always the same—always want to know right away what happened. Well, for starters, you're aboard the *Colonel Bowie*. You're in sick bay. Bet you figured that much out for yourself."

Oh boy. This one's going to be a laugh riot. I woke up in time to catch the comedienne's shift, Julian thought. Hey, did she say sick bay? Aboard the ship? I was in the middle of those Bugs, trying to get to Paolo . . .

"Guess you tried to take on the whole Bug warrior caste single-handed, eh, hero?"

"Unnnh . . ." It wasn't much to say, but at least he was getting better at it.

"Anyway, a couple of your friends are around here. I'll let them know Corporal Penn is now receiving."

Shortly, Julian heard Sutu's voice.

"Welcome back, Julian. On behalf of the squad, let me say we'd all like it more if you didn't feel obliged to fight this war single-handedly. Save a few Bugs for the rest of us next time, okay?"

"Ah, belay that garbage. He's a fine, strapping, fighting man, he is, and I'm proud to serve under him!" Brennan's booming tones almost drowned out Sutu's laughter. "How are you feeling, Julian?"

"Unnnh . . ."

"Well, now, the nurse said you'd probably say something like that," drawled Wade. "Looks like you're going to have an easy time of it on the way back to Sanctuary. Just think, you won't have to clean equipment, won't have to listen to us complain. You can just lie here and take it easy for three whole days.''

"Seriously, Julian," Sutu cut in. "How much information do you want to absorb right now? The docs say the answer to that question is up to you.''

"Mission . . .''

"Right. Our mission was successfully accomplished. The special talent made it. He's on board with us, being debriefed by a special mission team," Sutu replied. "Next?''

"Paolo?''

"A very lucky M.I. He was merely knocked unconscious by the mine. Even though his armor was virtually destroyed, Private Guiterez sustained only superficial wounds. Wade and I were able to make pickup on both of you after the Bugs took you down. No doubt you'll want to speak with him as soon as your condition improves.''

It didn't take much genius, even in Julian's pain-wracked condition, to notice the caution in Sutu's voice or the too-obvious fact that Paolo had chosen not to attend this little squad get-together. Julian summoned his strength to speak.

"Private Sutu. Has Private Guiterez made any statement concerning the action in our last drop?''

"Ah, now, let's get on to more pleasant things, shall we," Wade broke in. "Guess we ought to tell Penn here that he's been breveted to sergeant rank.''

"That's hardly more pleasant," Brennan commented.

Sutu read Julian the message relayed from the *Alvin York*:

FROM: Third Lt. Abram Weiss, aboard *Alvin York*
TO: Corporal Julian Penn, aboard *Colonel Bowie*
RE: Immediate Orders

Be advised I am now acting commander of Second Platoon, Company E, First Battalion, Second Regiment, First Mobile Infantry Division.

Upon arrival Sanctuary, take temporary command of second section of platoon with brevet rank of sergeant and await further orders.

Good work.

Julian groaned. He felt no elation as he read the message. His breveting to section command could mean only one thing: both Sergeant Stakowski and the assistant section leader had bought the farm. Stakowski had been a good man, a good friend, even if he was a sergeant. Even worse, a third lieutenant was in temporary command of the platoon. That meant the entire higher chain of command had gone down, given the supreme sacrifice. And Julian had a smart mouth like Paolo to deal with.

"Sutu. What about Paolo?"

"Is your inquiry official, Sergeant?" Sutu asked.

Julian thought hard about his answer. Paolo had definitely violated orders in a combat situation. His behavior endangered the mission and the squad. Obviously, from Sutu's cautious manner, Paolo had shot his mouth off afterward—*after I got myself put in this hospital trying to pull his fat out of the fire. There are three things I can do: thrash the jerk privately when I get out of here, report him up the chain of command for a general court-martial, or do nothing. If I answer yes to Sutu's question, it's a general court-martial for sure, and odds are Paolo will end up dancing Danny Deever at the end of a rope when we make Fleet Base at Sanctuary.*

If Julian chooses a court-martial for Paolo, go to section 14.

If Julian chooses to duke it out with Paolo, go to section 13.

If Julian chooses to do nothing, go to section 12.

— 7 —

Paolo was very, very lucky. He'd landed point-blank on a Bug mine and lived to tell about it. His armor was in tatters, but the crazy Latin had taken nothing worse than a bump on the head and a few superficial cuts. Apparently his jets had kicked in at the same time the mine went off. Lucky indeed.

Sutu and Wade had shown up on the bounce and fought like demons. After a taste of their flamers and HE bombs, the Bug brain had apparently thought better of this little skirmish. The Bug warriors scurried down their holes. Sutu stripped Paolo out of his armor while Julian dropped bombs down the Bug holes. There was no point in retrieving Paolo's armor. It was a total loss, and one man in powered armor can easily carry another who is out of his suit.

There was only one hitch with the pickup. Private James Wade of the Mobile Infantry perished in the fight.

Sutu carried Paolo to the retrieval boat while Julian covered their rear, just in case the Bugs staged a reappearance. "Board retrieval boat!" Julian ordered when they arrived. He was the last one up the ramp. He threw himself onto a launch cot as the boat's thrusters kicked in. Somehow, the boat pilot and the mother ship pilot managed to work a couple of miracles between them, and within twenty minutes Julian's squad, minus Wade, were safely aboard the *Colonel Bowie*.

Julian reported forward to the ship's captain and got the word on the operation. Apparently, the Bugs were expecting company. They must have spotted the special talent some time ago, because they were lying in wait to ambush his retrieval force. Thanks to Julian's squad, the special talent had gotten away safely. In fact, he was in another part of the ship right now, being debriefed by a special mission team composed of very hush-hush, tight-lipped intelligence types. The squad would have the M.I. quarters on the *Colonel Bowie* to themselves for the voyage back to Fleet Base on Sanctuary. The rest of the battalions were jammed aboard the *Alvin York*. The *Colonel Bowie* had taken several direct hits during the drop, and only one of her boats had been functional to make retrieval.

Overall, casualties had been heavy. Ten percent of the men were hit in their capsules on the way down. Somehow, the Bug missile-guidance system had gotten lucky against all the radar chaff those capsules threw off in descent. The captain could only spare five minutes' time to brief Julian; she had a ship to run. But before she dismissed him, the captain handed Julian a subspace message:

FROM: Third Lt. Abram Weiss, aboard *Alvin York*
TO: Corporal Julian Penn, aboard *Colonel Bowie*
RE: Immediate Orders

Be advised I am now acting commander of Second Platoon, Company E, First Battalion, Second Regiment, First Mobile Infantry Division.

Upon arrival Sanctuary, take temporary command of second section of platoon with brevet rank of sergeant and await further orders.

Good work.

Julian felt no elation as he read the message. His breveting to section command could mean only one thing: both Sergeant Stakowski and the assistant section leader had bought the farm.

Julian went aft, fighting back tears of anger and sorrow. Stakowski had been a good man, a good friend, even if he was a sergeant. The news would certainly demoralize the squad. Even worse, a third lieutenant was in temporary command of the platoon. That meant the entire higher chain of command had gone down, given the supreme sacrifice.

Not to mention Jim Wade, one his own men. Julian felt as responsible for Wade's death as if he had killed the man himself. If I hadn't let Paolo get out of line, Wade would still be alive, Julian thought.

As he rounded the corner to M.I. quarters, a voice stopped Julian in his tracks. It was Sutu's voice, drifting down the corridor.

"Yes. I'm sure you were doing everything by the book, Paolo. That's why Penn had to go off looking for you." Sutu, as always, was calm and deliberate, choosing his words with care. "You are quite fortunate your wounds were superficial and that we weren't all killed trying to rescue you from your own folly."

"That's right, you crazy Latin!" Brennan joined in. The big, burly Brennan was seldom as careful as Sutu about what he said. Brennan had a temper, and even M.I. training hadn't yet taught him to master it. "You almost got us all killed, and for nothing! Jim Wade died so you could stick your nose in a Bug hole!"

"Oh yeah, man? Well, you stow it, man," Paolo shouted back in his best self-righteous tone. "When the Bugs wipe out your hometown, you come tell me how it feels. You come tell me how you're not going to stick your nose down every Bug hole you can until those black horrors are eradicated. By the book, my boot! Penn can speak for himself. If he isn't man enough to chew me out himself, you won't do any good trying to do it for him. Besides, the man was out of control. If he'd been on the bounce, we'd have made it back fine, in plenty of time. He was supposed to be in command. He can pay the bill for Wade's farm, not me."

Paolo turned to see what Brennan and Sutu were staring at. His eyes met Julian's.

"Yeah, so, I say the same thing to your face, man," Paolo barked, toughing it out.

I have three real options, Julian thought. Oh, I can do what I want to do more than anything in the world: thrash this ungrateful jerk here and now, in front of Sutu and Brennan. But that's not an option for a squad commander. I can thrash him in private; that's the M.I. tradition. Or I can call for a general court-martial. Doesn't this fool know that disobeying orders in combat is a capital offense? If I say the word, he'll be dancing Danny Deever at the end of a rope before we've spent twelve hours in Sanctuary. Or, I can do nothing.

If Julian decides to thrash Paolo in private, go to section 13.

If Julian decides to bring Paolo up before a court-martial, go to section 14.

If Julian decides to ignore Paolo's behavior, go to section 12.

Regardless of Julian's decison, lower the squad's Morale by 1 for participation in a disastrous engagement and loss of a squad member.

— 8 —

Paolo was very, very lucky. He'd landed point-blank on a Bug mine and lived to tell about it. His armor was in tatters, but the crazy Latin had taken nothing worse than a bump on the head and a few superficial cuts. Apparently his jets had kicked in at the same time the mine went off. Lucky indeed.

Sutu and Wade had shown up on the bounce and fought like demons. After a taste of their flamers and HE bombs, the Bug brain had apparently thought better of this little skirmish. The Bug warriors scurried down their holes. Julian stripped Paolo out of his armor, tossed a few bombs down the Bug holes, and headed for the retrieval boat, carrying Paolo's unconscious form. There was no point in retrieving Paolo's armor. It was a total loss, and one man in power armor can easily carry another who is out of his suit.

There was only one hitch with the pickup. Privates James Wade and Matsusu Sutu of the Mobile Infantry perished in the fight, victims of the Bugs' last, explosive present before their retreat.

Julian handed Paolo to a crewman inside the retrieval boat, then threw himself onto a launch cot just as the boat's thrusters kicked in. Somehow, the boat pilot and the mother ship pilot managed to work a couple of miracles between them, and within twenty minutes Julian's squad, minus Wade and Sutu, were safely aboard the *Colonel Bowie*.

Julian reported forward to the ship's captain and got the word on the operation. Apparently, the Bugs were expecting company. They must have spotted the special talent some time ago, because they were lying in wait to ambush his retrieval force. Thanks to Julian's squad, the special talent had gotten away safely. In fact, he was in another part of the ship right now, being debriefed by a special mission team composed of very hush-hush, tight-lipped intelligence types. The squad would have the M.I. quarters on the *Colonel Bowie* to themselves for the voyage back to Fleet Base on Sanctuary. The rest of the battalions were jammed aboard the *Alvin York*. The *Colonel Bowie* had taken several direct hits during the drop, and only one of her boats had been functional to make retrieval.

Overall, casualties had been heavy. Ten percent of the men were hit in their capsules on the way down. Somehow, the Bug missile-guidance system had gotten lucky against all the radar chaff those capsules threw off in descent. The captain could only spare five minutes to brief Julian; she had a ship to run. But before she dismissed him, the captain handed Julian a subspace message:

FROM: Third Lt. Abram Weiss, aboard *Alvin York*
TO: Corporal Julian Penn, aboard *Colonel Bowie*
RE: Immediate Orders

Be advised I am now acting commander of Second Platoon, Company E, First Battalion, Second Regiment, First Mobile Infantry Division.

Upon arrival Sanctuary, take temporary command of second section of platoon with brevet rank of sergeant and await further orders.

Good work.

Julian felt no elation as he read the message. His breveting to section command could mean only one thing: both Sergeant Stakowski and the assistant section leader had bought the farm.

Julian went aft, fighting back tears of anger and sorrow. Stakowski had been a good man, a good friend, even if he was a sergeant. The news would certainly demoralize Brennan. Even worse, a third lieutenant was in temporary command of the platoon. That meant the entire higher chain of command had gone down, given the supreme sacrifice.

Not to mention Jim Wade and Matsusu Sutu, his own men. Julian felt as responsible for their deaths as if he had killed the men himself. If I hadn't let Paolo get out of line, they would still be alive, Julian thought.

As he rounded the corner to M.I. quarters, a voice stopped Julian in his tracks. It was Brennan's voice, drifting down the corridor.

"That's right, you crazy Latin!" Brennan shouted. The big, burly Brennan was seldom careful about what he said.

Brennan had a temper, and even M.I. training hadn't yet taught him to master it. "You almost got us all killed, and for nothing! Jim Wade and Matsusu Sutu died so you could stick your nose in a Bug hole!"

"Oh yeah, man? Well, you stow it, man," Paolo shouted back in his best self-righteous tone. "When the Bugs wipe out your hometown, you come tell me how it feels. You come tell me how you're not going to stick your nose down every Bug hole you can until those black horrors are eradicated. By the book, my boot! Penn can speak for himself. If he isn't man enough to chew me out himself, you won't do any good trying to do it for him. Besides, the man was out of control. If he'd been on the bounce, we'd have made it back fine, in plenty of time. He was supposed to be in command. He can pay the bill for Wade and Sutu, not me."

Paolo turned to see what Brennan was staring at. His eyes met Julian's.

"Yeah, so, I say the same thing to your face, man," Paolo barked, toughing it out.

I have three real options, Julian thought. Oh, I can do what I want to do more than anything in the world: thrash this ungrateful traitor here and now, right in front of Brennan. But that's not an option for a squad commander. I can thrash him in private; that's the M.I. tradition. Or I can call for a general court-martial. Doesn't this fool know that disobeying orders in combat is a capital offense? If I say the word, he'll be dancing Danny Deever at the end of a rope before we've spent twelve hours in Sanctuary. Or, I can do nothing.

If Julian decides to thrash Paolo in private, go to section 13.

If Julian decides to bring Paolo up before a court-martial, go to section 14.

If Julian decides to ignore Paolo's behavior, go to section 12.

Regardless of Julian's decision, lower squad Morale by 1 point for participation in a disastrous engagement and loss of squad members.

— 9 —

Hot flaming space! I pulled it off!

Julian suppressed these exuberant thoughts as he made for the retrieval-boat ramp. He couldn't help laughing out loud at Paolo, who was complaining in his finest Latino style.

"Hey man, take it easy! You took my armor off, remember? I'm not padded all around like you. My head is throbbing. You trying to kill me with the headache, man? Take it easy on these bounces!"

Paolo had been very, very lucky. He'd landed point-blank on a Bug mine, but lived to tell about it. His armor was in tatters, but the crazy Latin had taken nothing worse than a bump on the head and a few superficial cuts. Apparently his jets had kicked in at the same time the mine went off. Lucky indeed.

Julian had fought like a demon. After a taste of his flamer and HE bombs, the Bug brain had apparently thought better of this little skirmish. The Bug warriors scurried down their holes. Julian had stripped Paolo out of his armor, then dropped bombs down the holes after the retreating Bugs.

"Board retrieval boat!" Julian sang out happily. He was the last one up the ramp. He threw himself onto a launch cot as the boat's thrusters kicked in. Somehow, the boat pilot and the mother ship pilot managed to work a couple of miracles between them, and within twenty minutes Julian's squad were exchanging the usual post-action banter aboard the *Colonel Bowie*.

Julian reported forward to the ship's captain and got the word on the operation. Apparently, the Bugs were expecting company. They must have spotted the special talent some time ago, because they were lying in wait to ambush his retrieval force. Thanks to Julian's squad, the special talent had gotten away safely. In fact, he was in another part of the ship right now, being debriefed by a special mission team composed of very hush-hush, tight-lipped intelligence types. The squad would have the M.I. quarters on the *Colonel Bowie* to themselves for the voyage back to Fleet Base on Sanctuary. The rest of the battalions were jammed aboard the *Alvin York*. The *Colonel Bowie* had taken several direct hits during the drop, and only one of her boats had been functional to make retrieval.

Overall, casualties had been heavy. Ten percent of the men were hit in their capsules on the way down. Somehow, the Bug missile-guidance system had gotten lucky against all the radar chaff those capsules threw off in descent. The captain could only spare five minutes to brief Julian; she had a ship to run. But before she dismissed him, the captain handed Julian a subspace message:

FROM: Third Lt. Abram Weiss
TO: Corporal Julian Penn
RE: Immediate Orders

Be advised I am now acting commander of Second Platoon, Company E, First Battalion, Second Regiment, First Mobile Infantry Division.

Upon arrival Sanctuary, take temporary command of second section of platoon with brevet rank of sergeant and await further orders.

Good work.

Julian's elation was gone when he finished reading the message. His breveting to section command could mean only one thing: both Sergeant Stakowski and the assistant section leader had bought the farm.

Julian went aft, fighting back tears of anger and sorrow. Stakowski had been a good man, a good friend, even if he was a sergeant. The news would certainly demoralize the squad. Even worse, a third lieutenant was in temporary command of the platoon. That meant the entire higher chain of command had gone down, given the supreme sacrifice.

As he rounded the corner to M.I. quarters, a voice stopped Julian in his tracks. It was Sutu's voice, drifting down the corridor.

"Yes. I'm sure you were doing everything by the book, Paolo. That's why Penn had to go off looking for you." Sutu, as always, was calm and deliberate, choosing his words with care. "You are quite fortunate your wounds were superficial and that Julian wasn't killed trying to rescue you from your own folly."

"That's right, you crazy Latin!" Brennan joined in. The big, burly Brennan was seldom as careful as Sutu about what he said. Brennan had a temper, and even M.I. training hadn't yet taught him to master it. "You almost got Penn killed, and for nothing! So you could stick your nose in a Bug hole!"

"Oh yeah, man? Well, you stow it, man," Paolo shouted back in his best self-righteous tone. "When the Bugs wipe out your hometown, you come tell me how it feels. You come tell me how you're not going to stick your nose down every Bug hole you can until those black horrors are all dead meat. By the book, my boot! Penn can speak for himself. If he isn't man enough to chew me out himself, you won't do any good trying to do it for him. Besides, the man was out of control. If he'd been on the bounce, we'd have made it back fine, in plenty of time."

"Why, you ingrate!" Brennan roared. "That man saved

your life! He was as on the bounce as they come. The only thing he did wrong was engage in personal heroics—the rest of us could have come and helped—but right now, I'm almost glad we didn't. Why don't you and I—'' Brennan's tirade stopped in midsentence.

Paolo turned to see what Brennan, Sutu, and Wade were staring at. His eyes met Julian's.

''Yeah, so, I say the same thing to your face, man,'' Paolo barked, toughing it out.

I have three real options, Julian thought. Oh, I can do what I want to do more than anything in the world: thrash this ungrateful traitor here and now, in front of the whole squad. But that's not an option for a squad commander. I can thrash him in private; that's the M.I. tradition. Or I can call for a general court-martial. Doesn't this fool know that disobeying orders in combat is a capital offense? If I say the word, he'll be dancing Danny Deever at the end of a rope before we've spent twelve hours in Sanctuary. Or, I can do nothing.

If Julian decides to thrash Paolo in private, go to section 13.

If Julian decides to bring Paolo up before a court-martial, go to section 14.

If Julian decides to ignore Paolo's behavior, go to section 12.

— 10 —

''Yes, I have a suggestion,'' Julian said softly. ''Someone left the mats out on the gym floor. Would you like to help me clean them up?''

"Anything you say, Corporal," Brennan answered coldly.

The two men walked in silence to the ship's small exercise room. Brennan entered first. Julian followed him through the hatch, then locked it from the inside. The ship's crew could get in in case of an emergency; anyone else would take the hint.

"What rules, soldier?" Julian asked.

"Like I said, I don't want to kill you," Brennan replied. The man's face was still red with anger. "And I suppose I shouldn't injure you. There's a shortage of soldiers, and I wouldn't want the M.I. to be short one. That's assuming, of course, that you are a soldier."

"That's what this fight will determine, as far as you're concerned. *I* already know the answer," Julian answered calmly. "All right, then. Nothing lethal, no serious injuries."

"Agreed," said Brennan, and a half-second later his right fist almost took out Julian's front teeth. Almost, but not quite. Julian's head bobbed aside and Brennan's blow hit thin air. Julian's counterpunch might have ended the fight. For an instant, Brennan's face was forward, exposed, but he was a combat veteran, and his left arm blocked Julian's punch.

Wade and Sutu arrived outside the locked door in time to hear the thump of bodies hitting the mats. In the following minutes, that sound was repeated many times. There were also several *oofs* and more than one *unnh!*

"If Penn walks out, I'll buy the first round next time we're on leave," Wade commented.

"Penn has too much at stake. I'll buy if Brennan walks out. And to clarify, walks out unassisted," Sutu countered.

"Agreed."

It was fifteen minutes before the issue was settled. The locked hatch door opened. Brennan and Julian stood gasping, both leaning against the hatch for support, each holding up the other with his free arm. Both men looked worse than they had when boarding the retrieval boat after the Bug fight.

"Corporal Penn," Brennan grunted between deep breaths, "thank you for explaining the finer points of your command decision. As a fellow soldier, I appreciate your reasoning." It was the last thing Brennan said for eight hours.

"My pleasure," Julian managed to say as his eyes rolled upward. "Thanks for your help with those . . . mats . . ."

Wade carried Penn to his bunk, while Sutu lugged the unconscious Brennan to his.

"Well," Wade drawled as he and Sutu prepared to sleep, "looks like we'll be buying for them."

Go to section 15.

— 11 —

"Enough's enough, Brennan," Julian snapped. "We've all had our share of fighting for one day."

Brennan was closer to Paolo than any of the others, Julian thought. The man is overwrought. If I give him some time, he'll come around, Julian decided.

Brennan's eyes never left Julian's face until the corporal turned and left the room. Wade and Sutu sat on the edges of their bunks, and a silent message was exchanged with no more than a look.

"Yes, Corporal," Brennan finally said, speaking to no one. "Yes, we've all had enough fighting—except for you."

Lower the squad's Morale by 2 points and go to section 15.

— 12 —

"Oh, never mind," Julian said. He tried to suppress a sigh of disgust.

Paolo can wait until another day, he thought. We've all had enough fighting for today. Discipline can be handled when I feel more up to it.

Lower the squad's Morale by 2 points and go to section 15.

— 13 —

"Let's go, Paolo."

Julian had made his decision at once, but waited until the ship was nearing dock in Sanctuary to implement it. He knew Paolo recovered from lessons quickly; he wanted this one to last through the leave he expected the squad to get once the ship docked.

"Hey, man, anytime. Where we going?"

"Someone left the mats out on the gym floor. Would you like to help me clean them up?"

"Anything you say, man," Paolo answered coldly.

The two men walked in silence to the ship's small exercise room. Paolo entered first. Julian followed him through the hatch, then locked it from the inside. The ship's crew could get in in case of an emergency; anyone else would take the hint.

"What rules, soldier?" Julian asked.

"I don't want to kill you," Paolo replied, tossing his head arrogantly. "And I suppose I shouldn't injure you.

There's a shortage of soldiers, and I wouldn't want the M.I. to be short one."

"All right, then. Nothing lethal, no serious injuries," Julian answered calmly.

"Agreed," said Paolo, and a half-second later his right fist almost took out Julian's front teeth. Almost, but not quite. Julian's head bobbed aside and Paolo's blow hit thin air. Julian's counterpunch might have ended the fight. For an instant, Paolo's face was forward, exposed, but he was a trained M.I., and his left arm blocked Julian's punch.

Brennan walked past the locked door in time to hear the thump of bodies hitting the mats. In the following minutes, that sound was repeated many times. There were also several *oofs* and more than one *unnh!*

It was fifteen minutes before the issue was settled. The locked hatch door opened. Paolo and Julian stood gasping, both leaning against the hatch for support, each holding up the other with his free arm. Both men looked worse than they had when boarding the retrieval boat after the Bug fight.

"Corporal Penn," Paolo grunted between deep breaths, "thank you for explaining the finer points of your command decisions. As a fellow soldier, I appreciate your reasoning." It was the last thing Paolo said for eight hours.

"My pleasure," Julian managed to say as his eyes rolled upward. "Thanks for your help with those . . . mats . . ."

Brennan dragged both men to their bunks. Well, he thought, if that's what being a squad leader entails, I'm happy being a private, thank you.

Go to section 15.

— 14 —

Julian stood rigidly at attention as the band played "Danny Deever." I mustn't . . . I mustn't break down, not now, he thought. It took every ounce of his willpower to keep his jaw from trembling.

"Private Paolo Guiterez, stand forth," the major had said. "Private Guiterez, you are found guilty as charged. The court sentences you to be hanged by the neck until dead."

The automatic review of the court-martial record had taken three days. While most of the battalion—what was left of it—enjoyed liberty on Sanctuary, Julian kept to his duties, and to himself.

Did I make the right decision? Should I have just thrashed Paolo and let it go at that? The battalion commander remanded the case to a general court. He could have decided on a lighter, administrative punishment. But he's greener than new grass, and the battalion took a pasting in the raid on Birgu. A lot of good men were killed there obeying their orders. Paolo endangered lives and the accomplishment of the battalion's mission. He disobeyed a direct order in a combat situation. He put personal whim ahead of combat discipline.

No. I did the right thing, Julian decided. Now I·have to see it through.

The entire regiment passed in review at slow march. Paolo was led out to the gallows, and his uniform was stripped of all trace of insignia as the band played "Danny Deever." There was a drum roll. Paolo died.

That night, Julian reflected that duty is often hard, and liberty often costly. No one else in the barracks heard his stifled sobs.

Lower the squad's Morale by 1 point and go to section 15.

— 15 —

"All right, you apes. I don't know you, and you don't know me. The only thing we do know about each other is that we're all M.I., and we're all in this one together."

Julian studied the faces of his new men carefully, hoping that he somehow looked older, tougher, more experienced than the four bright, eager, green troopers staring back at him. My new squad, he thought. Oh well, they have to learn sometime. Hope they learn fast.

A stroke of an officer's pen had rearranged Julian's life instantly. The Second Battalion was being rebuilt on Sanctuary. Experienced men were at a premium. The old squad contained men who had been under fire, and men with even that little experience were badly needed to give new squads, filled with newly trained recruits, some combat seasoning. The squad had been broken up. Julian remained a squad leader instead of becoming a section leader, but he now commanded a squad of four untested, recently graduated trainees.

From a military point of view, green trainees have one virtue: they are expendable. And the high command had come up with a mission requiring one very expendable force. Julian's old squad had succeeded in retrieving the special talent in the recent botched drop on Birgu. This demonstrated some leadership potential on Julian's part. He was tapped to lead the almost-suicide mission.

The Skinnies were important allies for the Bugs. They provided the Bugs with some knowledge of humanoids and, more important, they provided the Bugs with humanoid-produced technology. No one knew what the Skinnies called themselves. The name was purely descriptive. Eight or nine feet tall, stick-thin and buck naked, the Skinnies were, nevertheless, closer relatives to the Terrans than to the Bugs. Why they sided with arachnids against humans was their business, and so were the details on exactly what items they provided to the Bugs. This mission would make that information the Federation's business as well.

The target: a Skinny industrial research-and-development facility on a major Skinny planet. At least, the Skinnies had the installation masked as an R&D facility. Federation officials were very interested to learn that the facility was, in fact, a Skinny "think-tank," a place where Skinnies with super brains planned Skinny military and diplomatic policy.

"A major raiding force wouldn't stand a chance," the lieutenant had explained to Julian. "Enough ships to carry a large force would alert their planetary defenses. A small force, a very small force, just might be able to sneak in, hit the think-tank, grab some prisoners, and get out. That's the mission."

"We're lucky. Most M.I. would give their eyeteeth for an important assignment like this," Julian told the new men. "A chance to provide very important prisoners, which could have a real bearing on the outcome of the war; that's what we have here," Julian said, hoping he was telling the truth. "Now, study this map carefully.

"Point A is our drop zone. It's fairly near the city's water plant at Point B—near enough that any local defenders will assume that's the target of our raid. The M.I. have made similar nuisance raids on several Skinny cities. Our raid will seem like a smaller version of the same old tactic. We'll feint toward the water tower, then rapidly turn toward the real target, Point C. It's a Skinny R&D facility where smart Skinnies think deep thoughts about Skinny plans. Once there, we overcome any local resistance, enter the facility, take prisoners, hold off any counterattack, and get retrieved right out of the plant's own transit facility.

"We don't know what the facility is like inside. Outside, there's a fenced perimeter, two armed guards at each of the two gates, and guard towers with substantial firepower at each of the corners. There are probably more

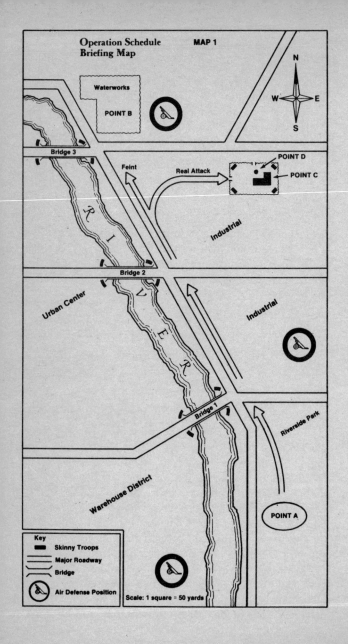

guards inside. The retrieval boat will land at Point D, right on their parking lot. Study both maps carefully.

"Above all, remember this: We've got a strict time limit. The retrieval beacon will sound seventeen minutes after we hit the ground, and the boat will land three minutes later. We have to be in position with prisoners waiting when that boat lands.

"Actual tactics for this operation will be worked out on the ground, depending upon the situation. I'll be in overall tactical command. This is strictly a one squad-raid; we're to fill up that retrieval boat with Skinny prisoners.

"One more thing. Some of you men may be a little nervous about making a daylight drop. I know it's unusual, and in combat the unusual can be frightening. Don't worry about it. The Skinnies will be so surprised to see us coming, they'll never be able to respond in time.

"That's it. You'll get reinforcement on these points during your hypno briefing during sleep," Julian concluded.

Julian's own sleep was fitful. He kept hoping he had told his men the truth about the daylight drop business. Besides, being in tactical command of a squad is one thing; being the senior officer on the ground is something altogether different, even if the mission involves only one squad of five men. When this drop began, Julian would be in command, on his own.

Julian awoke early, checked over the drop plan with the ship's officers, and readied himself mentally. At D-minus-thirty, he met his troops as they mustered in the drop room of the hastily repaired *Colonel Bowie*. Each man was suited up in powered armor, carrying a hand flamer, a large supply of ten-second fire pills, Y-rack with HE bombs, hand bombs, rocket launcher with HE warheads, and minimal survival gear.

"There's no chaplain with us on this drop," Julian said, "so we'll just take a moment of silence."

No one spoke in the stillness. Julian's own voice was the first to break the silence.

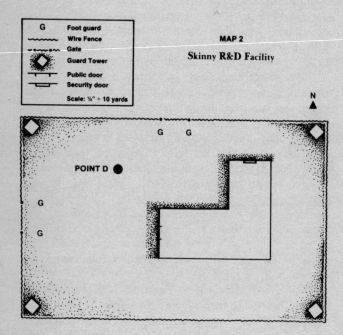

G	Foot guard
∿∿∿	Wire Fence
	Gate
◈	Guard Tower
	Public door
	Security door
Scale: ¼" = 10 yards	

MAP 2

Skinny R&D Facility

N ▲

POINT D ●

"Squad! Man your capsules!"

Julian watched as the four raw recruits were strapped into their multiskinned drop capsules, then received assistance from a Navy hand to strap into his own capsule.

"Bridge. Squad ready for drop," Julian reported. "Men, don't be nervous. This'll be just like your training drops, only this time we can strike a real blow."

"Good luck, Penn," the captain's voice came over Julian's headset.

Eight gees of force hit Julian as the ship suddenly braked in its orbit high over the Skinny world.

"Center line tube, fire!" the captain ordered. An explosion sounded all around Julian, then all was weightlessness, free fall toward the alien planet below. The capsule's skins burned away one by one in the planet's atmosphere. The braking chutes slowed the plunge, and then suddenly, Julian was falling alone in his powered armor, his last chute ready to be opened manually.

Julian checked on the position of his men, then scanned the ground below. There's the river, just like on the map, and there's the drop zone. Looks pretty crowded—there's some kind of Skinny gathering going on. Oh well, the map said it was a park.

On the west side of the river, Julian spotted the warehouse district and the urban center; on the east side, the industrial area. He picked out the water works plant to the north on the east bank.

Sunny day, Julian mused. Nice day for a picnic. Hmmm. Won't have any trouble bouncing around down there: flat terrain, with most of the buildings only one story high— about fifteen feet. The Skinnies built this city out, not up.

A flash of laser fire interrupted Julian's thoughts. Nuts! An air defense gun, on the west side of the river, just across from the drop zone! At least once we're down it can't hurt us much. And, uh oh. A Skinny military patrol heading south into town on the highway north of the target. They're reacting quickly, very quickly. Hope that patrol makes for the water plant.

Julian popped his last chute and drifted toward the park below. As he swiftly approached the ground, he could see the upturned, surprised faces of more than a hundred Skinny civilians. They were pointing and gawking as he dropped to within one hundred feet of the ground.

If Julian opens up on the civilians with fire pills and the hand flamer to scare them away, go to section 28.

If Julian lands and ignores the civilians, go to section 17.

Whatever Julian decides to do, record the following information about Julian's new squad:

Manpower: 5

Ordnance: 6 (rather than the standard 7; these are rookies)

Melee: 4 (rather than the standard 5)

Stealth: 7

Morale: Subtract 1 from the last recorded value for Julian's old squad. The new squad will have heard about him, so the old squad's Morale value transfers to the new squad. The Morale is being lowered by 1 to reflect the rookie status of this unit.

— 16 —

That was close, Julian thought, and it wasted valuable time. Where's the rest of the squad?

Julian flipped on his command beacon, visually scanned the sky for the rest of the squad, and began sending orders over his command circuit.

"Squad, home on my beacon and report. By the numbers! I don't have all of you on visual."

"Woczinski here, Corporal. I've landed on top of a warehouse on the west side of the river. Have you on visual. So does that Skinny air-defense gun crew."

"Miller here, sir. I'm about a hundred yards west of Woczinski. Sorry, sir, I mean, Corporal. I mean, you're not a 'sir,' exactly—"

"Quiet, Miller!" Julian snapped. "Estrada, where are you?"

"About another hundred yards west of Miller."

"LeClerc here. I'm on your side of the river, in the shrubs about two hundred yards behind you. The Skinny mob will be reporting to the local constabulary soon, and that air-defense gun is turning and leveling."

Great. Twenty minutes to get in and do the job and get out again, and they had to get dealt a sloppy drop. Julian dove for some nearby bushes just as a sheet of superhot light streaked through the very spot he was standing a second before. Great, thought Julian. Got to get the squad moving. But how? If we bounce, we're a target for that gun, and we could be spotted while in the air by the defense detachments the Skinnies have at the bridges. If we move along the ground, we've got civilians to contend with—mobs of them, and in daylight.

If Julian orders the squad to bounce, go to section 22.

If Julian orders the squad to move on the ground, go to section 25.

— 17 —

No use wasting ordnance on innocent civilians. Our mission here is to take those prisoners, not depopulate the city, Julian thought.

"Oof!"

Julian rolled as he hit the ground, released the final chute's cords, and sprang to his feet.

Someone shouted something in Skinny talk, and what a second before was a milling mass of gawking, silent civilians suddenly became a bloodthirsty mob! The Skinnies were coming for him, dozens of them. There's no choice but to fight, Julian thought, and it'll be hand to hand. They're too close now even to use the flamer.

Julian is alone; his Attack Strength is therefore only 4. Julian fights using Chart B.

Five Skinnies per round try to bring Julian down. As civilians, each Skinny has a Melee value of 1. The Skinnies fight using Chart F.

All Skinny casualties are immediately replaced from the mob at the start of the next round.

If Julian becomes a casualty in the first three rounds, go to section 29.

If Julian is still alive after three full rounds, go to section 30.

— 18 —

"Woczinski, take charge of Miller and Estrada. Knock out that air-defense gun position, then meet me at Bridge One," Julian ordered. "LeClerc, we head north to the east end of the bridge. Advance by alternating bounces. By the numbers. One!"

Julian readied his HE rocket launcher as LeClerc sailed past overhead. A rocket leapt from LeClerc's launcher.

"Two!" shouted Julian. He bounded over LeClerc. "Careful with those rocket launchers; we want to take that bridge intact. Need it to get the squad back together."

From the top of his bounce, Julian saw LeClerc's rocket slam into a slight ridge to the north of the bridge. As the smoke cleared, he could distinguish the outlines of a pillbox dug into the ridge. Obviously, the Skinnies were ready to defend this position.

"Change rhythm on our bounces," Julian radioed LeClerc. "Keep them guessing where we are. When we close, lay down covering fire with the flamers. I'll rush the pillbox and toss some bombs in."

Roll two six-sided dice. If the result is the same as or less than the squad's Stealth value (7), go to section 20.

If the result is greater than the Stealth value, go to section 21.

— 19 —

"Woczinski, take Miller and Estrada and sweep around in an arc. End up heading for the west end of Bridge One. LeClerc and I will head for the east end of the bridge. When you near the bridge, go to cover and contact me."

Julian's decision took less than ten seconds. His top priority was to get the squad together. That meant meeting by the bridge. Once the squad is reunited, Julian thought, I can worry about moving toward the real target of this messed-up drop.

Issuing orders while bouncing northward, roughly parallel to the river, Julian let fly some rockets and bombs, creating as much chaos as possible.

"LeClerc. There aren't any good targets in the park. Shift your Y-rack to scatter bombs in the warehouse region west of the river. Lay any rocket fire into the industrial region to the north of us, but don't hit the real target yet."

A few bounces later, Julian saw the low ridges on his side of the bridge. He also spotted Woczinski, Miller, and Estrada, bouncing toward the west end of the bridge. Skinny civilians jammed the streets, looking for safety. The warehouse section was burning nicely, and there was no sign of that Skinny patrol. Did it head for the waterworks?

At least, Julian thought, so far that air-defense gun hasn't killed any of us. Not for lack of trying, though.

Julian took cover on the east side of the road, just across from the bridge, and just in time. Laser fire erupted from the two ridges north and south of the mouth of the bridge, and two grenades landed on either side of him, throwing up clouds of dirt and debris.

"LeClerc! Take cover. There are two pillboxes on our side of this bridge!"

"And two on the other side as well, if those little ridges over there are like the little ridges over here," LeClerc answered. A second later, Julian saw him, crouching behind a small slope about fifty yards away.

"Woczinski here," a voice snapped in Julian's ear. "We're going to ground about two hundred yards from the bridge. There are two pillboxes, one on each side of the bridge. No idea how much firepower they've got."

Well, thought Julian, no one said it was going to be easy. The question is, do we take out these pillboxes? Or, do we just try to get Woczinski, Miller, and Estrada across? Taking them out would clean up our right flank but cost us time. A mad dash across the bridge might surprise the Skinnies and work, or it might cost me more than half my squad.

If Julian orders an attack on the pillboxes, with the object of taking out the Skinny positions, go to section 24.

If Julian orders his men to attempt a crossing under fire, go to section 27.

— 20 —

Julian lay flat on his belly, just east of the highway. Across the road he could see the pillbox, dug into the ridge at the southeast corner of the bridge. The Skinnies in there will be expecting something. Sure hope this works, Julian thought.

"Okay, bounce and fire on 'one,' I'll rush on 'two,' " he ordered LeClerc. Have to make a note to myself about LeClerc, he added to himself. He's certainly cool under fire.

"One!" Julian called.

Three seconds later the ridge erupted again as LeClerc's second rocket slammed into the pillbox. The explosion didn't seriously harm the position, but it created a lot of smoke and dust for cover. LeClerc sprayed into the flying debris with his hand flamer. Anything at all flammable in the air would create more smoke, provide more cover for Julian.

"Two!" Julian shouted. He flipped down his infrared snoopers so he could see clearly despite the smoke and rushed for the pillbox, two hand bombs at the ready.

Inside the tiny fortress, two Skinnies manned a pulse laser, a sort of laser "machine gun," while two others readied grenade launchers.

In the first round of combat, Julian and LeClerc have the advantage of the smoke-and-dust cover. They fire using Chart C. The four Skinnies can't see through the smoke and dust. They don't fire in the first round.

In the second and each following round:
Julian and LeClerc fire using Chart D.

The Skinnies fire using Chart D.

Continue the battle for four full rounds.

If Julian and LeClerc survive the first and kill all the Skinnies, go to section 31.

If Julian and LeClerc are killed, go to section 29.

If each side still has at least one survivor after the fourth round, go to section 23.

— 21 —

Julian lay flat on his belly, just east of the highway. Across the road he could see the pillbox, dug into the ridge at the southeast corner of the bridge. The Skinnies in there will be expecting something. Sure hope this works, Julian thought.

"Okay, bounce and fire on 'one,' I'll rush on 'two,' " he ordered LeClerc. Have to make a note to myself about LeClerc, he added to himself. He's certainly cool under fire.

"One!" Julian called.

Three seconds later the ridge erupted again as LeClerc's

second rocket slammed into the pillbox. The explosion didn't seriously harm the position, but it created a lot of smoke and dust for cover. LeClerc sprayed into the flying debris with his hand flamer. Anything at all flammable in the air would create more smoke, provide more cover for Julian.

"Two!" Julian shouted. He flipped down his infrared snoopers so he could see clearly despite the smoke and rushed for the pillbox, two hand bombs at the ready. Inside the tiny fortress, two Skinnies manned a pulse laser, a sort of laser "machine gun," while two others readied grenade launchers.

Julian and LeClerc failed their Stealth roll. Even though the smoke and dust provide some cover, they were seen "bouncing" into position by the air-defense laser on the west side of the river. It opens up as Julian dashes across the road.

The Skinnies have engaged with a total Manpower of 10 (four men in the pillbox and six with the air-defense gun). Their Ordnance value with the air-defense gun is 5 rather than the normal 3.

Julian and LeClerc fire using Chart D.

The Skinnies fire using Chart D.

The first M.I. hit is LeClerc, but he is only wounded and does not die until Julian is killed.

Continue the fight until all combatants on one side or the other are dead.

If Julian and LeClerc are killed, go to section 29.

If all the Skinnies are killed, go to section 31.

— 22 —

Better to risk the exposure and move on the bounce, Julian thought. It's faster that way, and that patrol I saw on the way down is already on the move.

"Squad, move on the bounce! You, west of the river, stay on the rooftops; the civilians in the streets will slow you down too much. LeClerc, alternate bounces with me. All others, alternate bounces, and set those buildings burning as you leave them. Make it look like a typical raid."

Even as he gave the orders, Julian analyzed the real problem. The squad is split: three men are west of the river, and the river is too wide to cross in one bounce.

Julian studied his memory of the map, implanted in his mind by hours of study and hypnotic reinforcement.

If Julian orders Woczinski, Miller, and Estrada to take out the air-defense gun position while he and LeClerc make for Bridge One, go to section 18.

If Julian orders the squad to make an immediate, concentrated attack on Bridge One, hitting it from both sides at once, go to section 19.

If Julian orders the squad to advance north along both sides of the river, heading for Bridge Two, go to section 26.

— 23 —

"Julian! Woczinski here. We're heavily engaged against this air-defense gun emplacement. It's dug in deep; we don't dare bounce and close with it. Anyone in the air will get picked off for sure."

Great, thought Julian. Just what I need to hear. We're completely pinned down by this pillbox, and the rest of my squad is cut off and getting nowhere fast. Meanwhile, time is slipping away.

If Julian orders Woczinski's group to make a last-ditch assault on the gun emplacement, while he (and LeClerc, if still alive) make a final attempt against the pillbox, go to section 32.

If Julian orders Woczinski's group to break off their attack and circle around behind the pillbox, go to section 33.

— 24 —

"Here's what we'll do. You men move as stealthily as possible into a position to take out the southernmost pillbox on your side. Miller and Estrada, lay down covering fire, kick up as much dust as possible. Woczinski, you rush the pillbox and lob in the bombs. As soon as they go off, all three of you go inside. LeClerc and I will follow a similar plan over on this side. When we've each cleared a pillbox, we'll move on the other two."

"Right, Julian. We're moving out now to take positions from which to rush the bridge. I'll signal when we're ready."

Woczinski sounded game enough, Julian thought.

"Miller here, Corporal Penn."

"Yes, Miller. What is it?"

"Corporal, I'm scared."

"So am I, Miller. So am I. Let's get it done, okay?"

"Uh, right, Corporal."

Julian considered poking his head up to watch down the length of the bridge, then decided against it. His tactical display showed the relative positions of his men. If they were spotted sneaking up to the pillboxes, he'd know it soon enough.

"LeClerc. Ready your rocket launcher. When they're in position, we want to bounce and put one rocket into each pillbox on our side of the river. I'll take the left one, you take the right. Then I'll rush the one to our left. The rockets should kick up enough dust to give me some cover."

"Okay. Hope the Skinnies on their side don't see them coming up. If they do, it could get real bad."

"Real bad I already know about. Now ready that weapon, soldier."

"But of course, *mon capitaine*."

Roll two dice. If the result is the same as or less than the squad's Stealth value, go to section 37.

If the result of the dice roll is greater than the squad's Stealth value, go to Section 39.

— 25 —

"Get on the ground and stay on the ground," Julian called over the command circuit. "Use fire pills to scatter civilians—make very low bounces to scatter them ahead of you. Use the cover of the buildings. We'll head north parallel to the river, just like in the original plan. Make toward Bridge Two. We'll find a way to get together there. Move!"

Julian started running for the north boundary of the park, the civilian mob just ahead of him.

Oh no! I'm going to overtake them, he thought.

Julian hit the dirt behind a low hill, still in the park and becoming more and more frustrated by the second.

"Better let that mob clear out, Julian."

"Right, LeClerc. While you're at it, lob a rocket or two toward the air-defense gun."

Thirty seconds ticked by. The mob cleared enough to allow Julian and LeClerc to progress. A single low bounce carried Julian across a major roadway into an industrial sector.

"Julian! They're swarming me!"

Julian upped the visual magnification. A quick look behind showed LeClerc swallowed up in a mob of civilians. The Skinnies were fleeing from their vehicles, abandoning them in the road he'd just crossed, and fleeing southward, away from the apparent advance of the M.I.

"Let 'em go by! They're panicked; I don't think they'll hurt you."

"Corporal Penn. Woczinski here. The streets are mobbed. We're going to have to make some short bounces over the rooftops to make any progress at all."

"Okay, okay, but stay out of the air as much as possible."

Watching for openings in the screaming mob, advancing whenever possible, Julian made his way north, staying just east of the riverside highway. LeClerc took up a position fifty to a hundred yards behind Julian.

Julian checked his tactical display and saw that Woczinski, Miller, and Estrada had become really bogged down in the warehouse district. He was pondering his next move when he spotted a Skinny on a nearby rooftop—a Skinny with some kind of walkie-talkie—looking right at him and LeClerc.

It's notifying that Skinny patrol!

The thought shot through Julian's mind like electricity. His hand flamer came up, he squeezed the trigger, the Skinny lookout evaporated in flames.

Can't take the risk that I got him in time, Julian thought. Have to get the squad together!

"Squad! Converge on Bridge One, both sides. Try to approach with stealth. Keep an eye out for Skinny defenders."

"Stealth! You've got to be kidding, Corporal. We're being mobbed over here. These civilians have turned nasty!" Estrada's voice was not reassuring. It had the tone of panic.

"Uh, yeah, Corporal. They're starting to turn on us. Some of them are firing weapons from the windows. What should we do?" Miller, too, seemed close to panic.

"All right, then, *bounce*! Let's go!"

Julian's first bounce showed him he'd ordered too little, too late. The Skinny patrol was already dividing up. Part of it was securing Bridge One, part was pouring into the warehouse district directly in front of Woczinski, Miller, and Estrada. The remainder of the patrol was heading right at LeClerc and Julian!

"Skinnies dead ahead. Let 'em have it!" Julian cried.

Roll two dice. If the result is the same as or less than the squad's Morale value, go to section 63.

If the result of the roll is greater than the squad's Morale value, go to section 66.

— 26 —

Julian's decision took only seconds. The original plan called for a feint to the north, he remembered. The idea was to make the Skinnies figure we're headed for their waterworks. Okay. We'll stay on both sides of the river and head north—maybe they'll think it's some kind of two-pronged attack. Meanwhile, we can wreak havoc, try to make our numbers look larger than they are. With luck, we'll draw that patrol right to the waterworks and they'll waste time taking up defensive positions there.

"Squad! We'll follow the original plan. Advance north,

parallel to the river, as far as Bridge Two. Use the buildings for cover. Stagger your bounces so the air-defense gunners can't predict where and when you'll next appear. We've got plenty of ammo. Use it, preferably on buildings. Avoid civilian casualties when possible, but sow havoc! Let's go, on the bounce!''

Julian's swift orders and solid reasoning were a tonic to the rookie troopers. Explosions began wracking the warehouse district, fires broke out, sirens wailed. At the top of each bounce, Julian saw more and more civilians jamming the streets, fleeing for underground shelters. He noted with approval that Woczinski, Miller, and Estrada were varying their bounce patterns as ordered.

"Whee, Corporal! I just got a big warehouse of some sort—must have been filled with petrochemicals!''

Even from the ground, Julian could see the flames shooting more than three hundred feet into the air from somewhere west of the river.

"Nice shooting, Miller. Keep moving!'' Julian called.

"Look Julian, pillboxes, just to the left, by the first bridge.''

LeClerc was definitely earning his pay today, Julian thought. I'll have to remember to buy him a dinner when this is over.

"Right. Head straight into the industrial buildings. They won't want to risk firing very low near their own complexes,'' he answered.

Julian's intuition to move "on the bounce'' instead of on the ground seemed to be paying off. The air-defense guns couldn't lock on their targets in time—the bouncing troopers were up in the air, then down among the buildings before the big guns could fire accurately.

Those pillboxes, though, could mean trouble, Julian realized. Midway through the first major industrial section, Julian risked an extra-high bounce, giving himself more time in the air to survey the defenses around the bridges. Bridge Two was just ahead, and it looked like a problem.

The natural-looking ridges by the bridge, two at each end, were probably Skinny pillboxes. If they're manned, Julian reasoned, we'll have a devil of a time getting Miller, Estrada, and Woczinski across that bridge. And we've got to get the squad back together.

"Julian, it's Woczinski. We're picking up scattered ground fire from our rear as we advance. Looks like Skinny troops from the pillboxes at Bridge One are following us through the urban center. No real trouble yet—we can outdistance them. But what should we do when we get to Bridge Two?"

"Wow! Let's storm that bridge!" The enthusiastic whoop came from Miller.

"Hey man, you crazy? Storm pillboxes? What you say, Julian?"

Good question, Estrada, Julian thought. The squad leader noted with pleasure that bombs from his Y-rack had just ignited a large section of what appeared to be a munitions factory. Then he turned his mind to an answer to Estrada's query.

If Julian decides to order Miller, Estrada, and Woczinski to rush across Bridge Two while he and LeClerc lay down covering fire, go to section 54.

If Julian orders the entire squad to advance north of Bridge Two on both sides of the river, then double back and try to cross it, go to section 53.

— 27 —

"Okay men, we're in a tight situation. Here's how we get out of it. LeClerc and I are in good positions on the east side of the bridge. Woczinski, Miller, Estrada—you have to inch your way forward to just under the noses of those pillboxes. When you're in position, let me know. LeClerc and I will start raising cain on this side. Then you three bounce for it—two or three bounces and you're across. On your last bounce, hit the dirt and we'll reorganize on this side of the river.''

Julian waited for a reply, but heard nothing. Across the river, Miller, Estrada, and Woczinski peered from behind a burning warehouse at the bridge. They could see the pillboxes despite the Skinnies' careless attempts at camouflage. They could also see the highway, forty yards wide with no cover, no cover at all. And they saw that highway stretching more than 150 yards across the river. They knew there would be more Skinnies waiting on the other side, no matter how good Julian and LeClerc were at laying down covering fire.

Roll two dice. If the result is the same as or less than the squad's current Morale value, go to section 38.

If the result of the dice roll is greater than the squad's current Morale value, go to section 44.

— **28** —

The lawn below Julian exploded into flames. The mass of stupefied Skinnies were no longer gawking; they were running for their lives. A handful of ten-second fire pills and one blast from the hand flamer, enough to clear the drop zone of civilians, Julian thought. Lucky for me, this old power armor can withstand the flames, no problem.

But now's no time to admire the flaming scenery.

Julian flipped on his command beacon, visually scanned

the sky for the rest of his squad, and began sending orders over his command circuit.

"Squad, home on my beacon and report. By the numbers! I don't have you on visual."

"Woczinski here, Corporal. I've landed on top of a warehouse on the west side of the river. Have you on visual. So does that Skinny air-defense gun crew."

"Miller here, sir. I'm about a hundred yards west of Woczinski. Sorry, sir, I mean, Corporal. I mean, you're not a 'sir,' exactly—"

"Quiet, Miller!" Julian snapped. "Estrada, where are you?"

"About another hundred yards west of Miller."

"LeClerc here. I'm on your side of the river, in the shrubs about two hundred yards behind you. That air-defense gun is turning and leveling."

Great. Twenty minutes and counting, and I got a messed up drop with soldiers spread all over the place. Julian dove for some nearby bushes just as a sheet of superhot light streaked through the very spot he was standing a second before. Great, thought Julian. Got to get the squad moving. But how? If we bounce, we're a target for that gun, and we could be spotted while in the air by the defense detachments the Skinnies have at the bridges. If we move along the ground, we've got civilians to contend with— mobs of them, and in daylight.

If Julian orders the squad to bounce, go to section 22.

If Julian orders the squad to move on the ground, go to section 25.

— 29 —

History is full of examples of the difference one man, or one group of men, can make. Although their names never appeared in the history books, Julian and his men did live on in the textbooks. Future generations of M.I. officers studied his mistakes. Perhaps it was one such officer who remembered Julian Penn and led his men to victory over the Skinnies. It *is* documented in the history books that the Skinnies changed sides, gave support to the Terran Federation, and allowed Humans to triumph over Bugs . . . at least for a while.

You can return to section 1 and try again.

— 30 —

Julian fought like a wildcat. The Skinnies went sprawling left and right with crushed sternums and other fatal blows. Unarmed civilians aren't any match against a trained M.I. trooper in a ton of powered armor. Still, thought Julian, one wrong step could knock me down, and a smart Skinny could start ripping me out of my shell. . . .

Flames exploded from the midst of the mob milling and screaming around Julian. A second gush of fire ripped through the mob, and the Skinnies fled in panic.

Julian whirled around, switched to infrared scanning, and spotted LeClerc, flamer in hand, crouched in some nearby bushes.

"Thanks, pal" Julian called over the squad circuit.

Go to section 16.

— 31 —

Julian lay in the dust and rubble inside the remains of the Skinny pillbox.

"Looks like we've captured a few weapons," LeClerc said. Julian couldn't see the grin on LeClerc's face, but he heard it in his tone of voice.

"Great. Now all we need to do is get on with this fouled-up mission." Julian hoped the humor in his own voice wasn't too grim.

"By the way, I'm sure you noticed that there are three more Skinny pillboxes: one just to the north on this side of the bridge and two on the opposite side. Looks like they intended to hold this position against any raiding force," LeClerc commented.

"Right. Well, the ones in this pillbox failed to live up to expectations," Julian replied, switching his comm unit circuit to talk to the entire squad. "Woczinski, what's happening at your end?"

"We're under cover. That air-defense gun position is heavily guarded, well dug in. If we bounce toward it, we'll be picked off for sure."

"Any casualties there?"

"None of ours hit. We've lobbed rockets at the gun position. I can't say whether we damaged the Skinnies or not."

Julian pondered his options, then gave orders, hoping he'd made the right choice and that the uncertainty he felt hadn't come through in his voice.

If Julian orders Woczinski's group to hold position, and tries to get himself and LeClerc across the bridge to join them, go to section 35.

If Julian orders Woczinski's group to break off combat

with the gun position and circle around to the east end of the bridge, go to section 36.

— 32 —

"Okay, so we've got a few problems. Nothing that some good hard fighting and a lot of raw nerve can't solve," Julian snapped to the entire squad.

"You on the gun position. It's got to be taken out. If we don't get it, it will probably get our retrieval boat. I'll make a new effort here at the bridge. Let's get moving."

Unfortunately, Julian had let desperate enthusiasm get the better of his judgment. He bounced high, slamming another rocket into the pillbox, only to see laser fire erupting from all around the bridge. He had time to see Woczinski, also high in the air, literally cut in half by a direct hit from the air-defense gun. He even had time to see Skinnies emerging, firing lasers and grenade launchers, from the three other pillboxes in the area of the bridge. He felt a numbing shock, then searing pain, and then all went black.

Go to section 29.

— 33 —

"Okay, Woczinski, here's the new plan." Julian spoke calmly, hoping his growing concern didn't show in his voice. "Break off your attack on the gun position—melt away as best you can. Make for the east end of the bridge. We'll attack as a united squad, take the bridge from both ends at once. LeClerc and I will lay low until you're in position.''

Best way to take a bridge, Julian thought, is from both ends at once. But wait! Why take the bridge? All I really need to do is get Woczinski's group over to this side!

The Skinnies ceased firing just as Julian was framing a new plan. The silence was deafening. Evey normal background sound took on new significance, presented a new threat. Were more Skinnies moving into position? Were those vehicle sounds normal traffic? Civilians heading for a safer area? Or were they sounds of that Skinny patrol making for this fight?

"We're in position now, Julian." Woczinski's voice was low, calm, confident. "There are two pillboxes on our side of the bridge: one just to the north and one just to the south. I can't make out how much firepower they have inside, but those bunkers look like they could take a lot of pounding. The enemy hasn't spotted us yet; at least, they aren't shooting at us. What's the order?''

"Okay. I'm just across the bridge from you. Now listen, there's no use taking this bridge—we don't need it to get back, and we don't need casualties! When I give the word, you guys advance across that bridge, on the bounce! Go for all you're worth and take cover as soon as you get to this side. I'll lay down covering fire. You guys fire as you bounce, mainly for cover and distraction. Let your Y-racks do most of the work. Everybody got it?''

"Got it," Woczinski snapped.

"Sounds good to me," Estrada chimed in cheerfully.

"Uh, okay, gee, uh, I'm a little,—"

"Yeah, Miller. I'm scared, too. Now let's do our job," Julian cut in confidently. "*Now!* Move, move, move!''

Julian was in the air, high in a bounce. He slammed one rocket toward the nearest pillbox, scattered a handful of fire pills for distracting effect, and saw Estrada bounce into the air on the far side of the bridge. Then, everything erupted at once. The Skinnies in both pillboxes on the far side opened fire; so did those on Julian's side of the river. Another group of Skinnies emerged from the fourth pillbox, north of the bridge on Julian's side. They were coming into the open, firing!

Calculate the Attack Strength for both sides. There are twelve Skinnies firing, plus any Skinnies left in the pillbox first attacked by LeClerc and Julian. Skinnies have an Ordnance value of 3.

Skinnies fire using Chart D.

Julian's squad fires using Chart E.

Continue the fight for only five rounds. Then the Skinnies left run.

If all of Julian's squad are killed, go to section 29.

If Julian and one or more other squad members survive, go to section 40.

If Julian is the sole M.I. survivor, go to section 42.

— 34 —

The next seconds were a nightmare for Julian. Laser fire everywhere; explosions from the bombs in the men's Y-racks; smoke, dust, debris, screams.

Julian rolled in the dirt, dodged a pulse laser blast, and turned in time to see Woczinski land beside him and take cover A bomb from Woczinski's Y-rack took out the last Skinny.

"All across that's coming across, Julian," Woczinski quipped.

Great, thought Julian. Now what?

Go to section 41.

— 35 —

"Woczinski, you and the men with you lie low. We're coming to give you a hand."

LeClerc shot Julian a glance, forgetting for the moment that Julian couldn't see the question in his eyes through the suit's faceplate.

"What are you looking at? Those men are green as grass and in a tight spot. We're going to rush across this bridge and help them out, that's all," Julian said.

"Ah, I see. We are the cavalry to the rescue. That explains it all, *mon commandant*. Forgive me; I merely hoped, for a brief moment, that *they* would be the cavalry."

"I tossed a coin. We lost. Now, let's inflict as much damage as possible getting across this bridge. We'll use rockets to kick up dust and debris, fire pills for smoke, and set our Y-racks on automatic. Got it?"

"But of course. Citizenship, here we come."

"Yeah. I'll go first, out that hole, then bounce. You follow when I'm at the top of my bounce. By the numbers from then on. Got it?"

"After you, Alphonse."

"Very funny."

Julian readied his rocket launcher, rolled through the hole in the concrete wall of the bunker, jumped to his feet, and bounced, slamming a rocket into one of the pillboxes on the far side of the bridge.

Too late! He was at the top of his bounce before he saw the Skinnies rushing the pillbox he and LeClerc had just taken!

Woczinski and his men tried in vain to raise Julian on the comm. When the retrieval beacon sounded, they headed for the pickup point, hoping to link up with Julian and the rest of the M.I. there. They were cut down before they reached the R&D complex, so no one was left to report on the total failure of the mission.

Go to section 29.

— 36 —

"Woczinski, here's the plan. Break off your attack on the gun position. Don't bounce away; drift away. Lay down a little fire toward the gun; try to make them think you're repositioning for another go at them. Then move as fast as you can toward the west end of Bridge One. Be careful as you approach. There are two pillboxes on your side of the river, one just north and one just south of the bridge. LeClerc and I are holding a similar pillbox on the east end, south side. When you're in good cover within rushing distance of the bridge, let me know."

"Got it." Woczinski's reply was firm and calm.

"LeClerc, listen up. We'll lay down covering fire from here. Maybe one of us will even rush out, just to draw some fire. As we do that, we'll have them storm the bridge from the other side. Our objective isn't to capture it—we don't have time and can't afford the casualties. All we want to do is get the squad back together so we can get on with the mission."

"Sounds good to me. How much time is left?"

LeClerc's question caught Julian off guard. Stupid! How could he have forgotten to keep careful track of the time? Julian checked his chronometer.

"Almost five minutes gone by—wasted time. If you see me wasting any more, say so."

"But of course, *mon capitaine*. And Julian, it's not your fault the drop got scattered."

"Yeah, but attacking the air-defense gun was stupid—a waste of time, and maybe worse. We'll soon know."

Julian checked his chronometer again. He watched the seconds ticking by; every one seemed like an hour.

"Julian!"

"Report, Woczinski."

"We're in perfect position! The pillboxes on our side are empty. Look on the bridge! The Skinnies are rushing you!"

Julian took a quick glance. It was too good to be true!

"Okay, men, let 'em have it! Fire and advance! By the numbers. LeClerc, limit yourself to the hand flamer—we don't want to fire into our own men coming across!"

"Don't worry. I'll get the four rushing at us from the rear. They must be from that pillbox just north of us!"

There are twelve Skinnies rushing Julian's pillbox, eight from the front (on the bridge) and four from the rear. Run this all as one large firefight.

The Skinnies fire using Chart E.

Julian's squad fires using Chart C.

Continue the fight until one side or the other is completely eliminated.

If Julian's squad wins the fight, but Julian is the sole survivor, go to section 43.

If Julian's squad wins, and at least one M.I. other than Julian is alive, go to section 34.

If Julian's squad is wiped out, go to section 29.

— 37 —

"Julian, we're ready."

"Good, Woczinski. How far are you from the bridge?"

"Not more than fifteen yards. As soon as we move, those pillboxes will spot us."

"Okay, when I give the word, lay down covering fire and then move out fast. Use rockets, one at each pillbox, before the rush.

Julian checked his own rocket launcher and hand flamer, then readied some fire pills.

"LeClerc. Ready?"

"Ready, Julian."

"Everybody, on my signal . . ."

Julian poked his head above the rise. He could clearly see the road in front of him and the two Skinny pillboxes facing him, waiting to spit death. Across the bridge, flames were devouring a section of the city. There was nothing else to see. Julian knew he'd spot the action on the other side at the top of his bounce. For an instant, he wondered if any of the Skinny civilians who had run from the park were watching, or maybe alerting that Skinny patrol. No time to worry now.

"Squad, *fire! Bounce!*"

Julian squeezed the first trigger on his rocket launcher. The rocket spotted the left pillbox and locked on target. Julian squeezed the second trigger, and the rocket leapt toward its target as he bounced forward, hand bombs ready.

Woczinski, too, leapt from his hiding place into the cloud of dust kicked up by Miller and Estrada's rockets.

There are a total of sixteen Skinnies firing at Julian's squad. Each Skinny has an Ordnance value of 3.

The Skinnies fire using Chart E for the first round of the battle and Chart D for every succeeding round.

Julian's squad fires using Chart C.

The fight lasts until all combatants on one side are killed.

If any squad member besides Julian is alive at the end of the combat, go to section 51.

If Julian is the only M.I. survivor, go to section 43.

If the squad is wiped out, go to section 52.

— 38 —

Woczinski's voice broke the silence.

"Right, Julian. We're moving out now to take positions from which to rush the bridge. I'll signal when we're ready."

"Miller here, Corporal Penn."

"Yes, Miller. What is it?"

"Corporal, I'm scared."

"So am I, Miller. So am I. Let's get it done, okay?"

"Uh, right, Corporal."

Julian considered poking his head up to watch down the length of the bridge, then decided against it. His tactical display showed the relative positions of his men. If they were spotted sneaking up to the pillboxes, he'd know it soon enough.

"LeClerc. Ready your rocket launcher. When they're ready, we want to bounce, and put one rocket into each pillbox on their side of the river. I'll take the left one, you take the right. The Skinnies on our side should be content to fire at us."

"Okay. Hope the Skinnies on their side don't see them coming up. If they do, it could get real bad."

"Real bad I already know about. Now ready that weapon, soldier."

"But of course, *mon capitaine*."

Roll two dice. If the result is the same as or less than the squad's Stealth value, go to section 45.

If the result of the roll is greater than the squad's Stealth value, go to section 47.

— 39 —

"Julian, we're ready."

"Good, Woczinski. How far are you from the bridge?"

"Not more than fifteen yards. As soon as we move, those pillboxes will spot us."

"Okay, when I give the word, lay down covering fire and then move out fast. Use rockets, one at each pillbox, before the rush."

Julian checked his own rocket launcher and hand flamer, then readied some fire pills.

"LeClerc. Ready?"

"Ready, Julian."

"Everybody, on my signal . . ."

Julian poked his head above the rise. He could clearly see the road in front of him and the two Skinny pillboxes facing him, waiting to spit death. Across the bridge, flames were devouring a section of the city. There was nothing else to see. Julian knew he'd spot the action on the other side at the top of his bounce. For an instant, he wondered if any of the Skinny civilians who had run from the park were watching, or maybe alerting that Skinny patrol. No time to worry now.

"Squad, *fire! Bounce!*"

Julian squeezed the first trigger on his rocket launcher. The rocket spotted the left pillbox and locked on target. Julian squeezed the second trigger, and the rocket leapt toward its target as he bounced forward, hand bombs ready.

Woczinski, too, leapt from his hiding place into the cloud of dust kicked up by Miller and Estrada's rockets. Then disaster struck. The pillboxes spat death, and an air-defense gun on the east side of the river suddenly opened up as well. In an instant, Julian knew what had happened. The Skinnies had spotted Woczinski's group moving up, radioed for fire support from the gun, and waited for the M.I. to make their move!

There are a total of twenty-two Skinnies firing at Julian's squad: sixteen in the pillboxes and six manning the east-side air-defense gun. Each Skinny has an Ordnance value of 4 rather than the usual 3. This reflects the higher firepower of the gun.

The Skinnies fire using Chart D.

Julian's squad fires using Chart D.

The fight lasts until all combatants on one side are killed.

If Julian's squad kills all the Skinnies, and there are any surviving M.I. in addition to Julian, go to section 51.

If Julian is the sole M.I. survivor, go to section 43.

If the squad is wiped out, go to section 52.

— 40 —

The next seconds were a nightmare for Julian. Laser fire everywhere; explosions from the bombs in the men's Y-racks; smoke, dust, debris, screams.

Julian rolled in the dirt, dodged a pulse laser blast, and turned in time to see Woczinski land beside him and take cover.

"All across that's coming across, Julian," Woczinski quipped.

Great, thought Julian. Now what?

Go to section 41.

— 41 —

"We've wasted enough time. Squad, move out straight toward the target, northeast, through the industrial sector. Alternate bounces, throw some bombs from your Y-racks behind you, but avoid firing forward. I don't want them to get our bearing. Go to ground at approximately two hundred yards and await further instructions."

Julian spotted trouble on his fifth bounce—and he wasn't the only one to spot it.

"Skinny patrol! It's heading right down the minor streets toward us. They've spotted us," Woczinski called.

"I see them."

Yes, I *see* them, Julian thought. Now, what am I going to *do* about them?

The Skinny patrol were regulars, a tougher bunch than the old vets manning the bridge pillboxes. At the top of his next bounce, Julian tried to count the enemy. At least four vehicles, maybe more, four Skinnies to a vehicle. Their weaponry included laser rifles for each trooper, grenade launchers, and pulse lasers mounted on the vehicles.

The Skinnies were watching Julian even as he watched them. Two of the vehicles suddenly stopped and, two Skinnies jumped out and headed for the buildings. Julian realized they were probably going for the rooftops, where they could get a better shot at his bouncing M.I. troopers.

This large industrial area resembled one of the old industrial parks on Terra, before most of the manufacturing was moved offplanet, closer to the sources of raw materials. Flat land was covered with long, low buildings in odd shapes. Plenty of open area was left for vehicle transportation, parking, and loading. There were several obstacles to avoid during a bounce, especially the high wire fences.

Julian lobbed a bomb at one of the buildings a Skinny trooper had entered. He considered his options.

He could have the men go to ground and engage in some old-fashioned street fighting. That would minimize the danger of being shot while in the air. It would also slow their advance to the real target. Or, he could brazen it out, approach the target building on the bounce, just as if the squad intended to bounce right over it and keep going. Then, at the last second, the squad would stop and dash inside to round up prisoners.

Whatever I do, I'd better do it soon, Julian thought as the first Skinny laser fire narrowly missed him.

If Julian orders the squad to approach the target on the ground, fighting the Skinny patrol in the streets as they advance, go to section 68.

If Julian orders the squad to advance toward the target on the bounce, taking potshots at the Skinnies as they advance, go to section 69.

— 42 —

Wiped out! Oh no, what have I done!

Not even his power suit's environmental controls could stop the flood of tears that Julian shed. The bridge crossing was sheer carnage. Laser fire everywhere; explosions from the men's Y-rack bombs; smoke, dust, debris, screams, and, in the end, death. They were all dead.

Except me, Julian thought as he slid another rocket into the launcher. Like a robot following a program, he checked his hand flamer and set the Y-rack for automatic.

All dead except me. Well, you skinny bastards, Julian Penn is M.I., and cap troopers don't die easily!

Julian leapt to his feet and bounced high in the air, firing again: first the rocket, then the hand flamer. The Skinnies were all around him.

Julian felt fire—pure, cleansing, grief-burning fire—spread through his body, and his world turned black.

Go to section 29.

— 43 —

Wiped out! Oh no, what have I done!

Not even his power suit's environmental controls could stop the flood of tears that Julian shed. The bridge crossing was sheer carnage. Laser fire everywhere; explosions from the men's Y-rack bombs; smoke, dust, debris, screams, and, in the end, death. They were all dead.

Except me, Julian thought as he slid another rocket into the launcher. Like a robot following a program, he checked his hand flamer and set the Y-rack for automatic.

The Skinny patrol had showed up just as the last of Julian's original Skinny foes went down. Now, Julian thought, it's time to show what I'm made of.

All dead except me. Well, you Skinny bastards, Julian Penn is M.I., and cap troopers don't die easily!

Julian leapt to his feet and bounced high in the air, firing again: first the rocket, then the hand flamer. The Skinnies were all around him.

Julian felt fire—pure, cleansing, grief-burning fire—spread through his body, and his world turned black.

Go to section 29.

— **44** —

Miller's voice broke the long silence.

"Corporal Penn, I . . . that is, we . . . well, that bridge is awful far across. You know? If you don't mind, why don't we just knock out these pillboxes first?"

"Woczinski here. Julian, we think your order sounds like suicide. How about it?"

Disaster, thought Julian, absolute disaster. They're not disobeying, they're questioning. That means they've lost confidence in me, and they're losing confidence in themselves. We've got eighteen minutes left to accomplish our mission. Problem is, they're afraid of being shot at. Better let them get used to the idea. Time enough to worry about discipline later, back aboard ship.

"Okay," Julian heard himself say. "We'll do it your way this time."

Go to section 24.

— 45 —

"Julian, we're ready."

"Good, Woczinski. How far are you from the bridge?"

"Not more than fifteen yards. As soon as we move, those pillboxes will spot us."

"Okay, when I give the word, bounce for that bridge. Set your Y-racks on automatic; they'll drop grenades behind you as you come. Don't move out until I tell you. Miller?"

"I'm all right, Julian."

Now that action is imminent, Miller seems calmed down, Julian thought. He checked his own rocket launcher and hand flamer, then readied some fire pills.

"LeClerc. Ready?"

"Ready, Julian."

"You and I bounce on my signal."

Julian poked his head above the rise. He could clearly see the road in front of him and the two Skinny pillboxes facing him. Across the bridge, flames were devouring a section of the city. There was nothing else to see. Julian knew he'd spot the pillboxes on the other side at the top of his bounce. For an instant, he wondered if any of the Skinny civilians who had run from the park were watching, or maybe alerting that Skinny patrol. No time to worry now.

"LeClerc, *bounce*!"

Julian leapt skyward and forward. He squeezed the first trigger on his rocket launcher at the top of his bounce. The rocket spotted the rear of the left pillbox across the river and locked on target. Julian squeezed the second trigger, and the rocket leapt toward its target as he descended near the left pillbox on his own side of the river.

"Now, squad! Move, move, *move*! On the bounce!"

Woczinski, Miller, and Estrada leapt from their hiding places, grenades spewing from their Y-racks and arcing behind them.

There are a total of sixteen Skinnies firing at Julian's squad. Each Skinny has an Ordnance value of 3.

The Skinnies fire using Chart D.

Julian's squad fires using Chart C.

The combat lasts for only four rounds. Then the Skinnies run.

If any squad members besides Julian are alive at the end of the combat, go to section 46.

If Julian is the only M.I. survivor, go to section 43.

If the squad is wiped out, go to section 48.

— 46 —

There's thirty seconds I'll never forget, Julian thought as he lay panting in the dirt.

The Skinnies had been surprised, but they caught on real quick. They were firing by the time Julian gave the order for Woczinski, Miller, and Estrada to rush across the bridge. It seemed to Julian as though everything had happened in slow motion. He could still see his three men emerging from the smoke in the middle of the bridge, bouncing high. He could see the laser fire directed at him from the east-side pillboxes. The grenade explosions were almost deafening. The Skinnies in the pillboxes had grenade launchers, and their ordnance added to the din of the bombs tossed from the M.I.'s Y-racks.

The Skinnies on the west side of the bridge were no dopes either. As soon as Woczinski and company had made their dash, those Skinnies darted out of their pillbox, swinging one of their pulse lasers around with them. That thing had sent a stream of laser fire right down the length of the bridge, barely missing his men.

I'm not even sure how many Skinnies are left, Julian mused, but now's not the time to worry about that. Got to get moving. Question is, which way? North along the river, feinting as planned, or straight across the industrial sector to the target? Only fifteen minutes left; this choice had better be the right one!

"Hey, Julian, which way do we go?"

Woczinski shouted the question as he rolled down an embankment. Half a second later, the top of the embankment exploded in flames. Clearly, there were still some Skinnies capable of shooting.

Add 1 point to the squad's Morale. Then deduct 1 point from Morale for each squad member killed. Remember, squad Morale can never be higher than 10.

If Julian orders the squad north, parallel to the river, as in the original mission plan, go to section 49.

If Julian orders the squad to move out directly toward the target, go to section 50.

— **47** —

"Julian, we're ready."

"Good, Woczinski. How far are you from the bridge?"

"Not more than fifteen yards. As soon as we move, those pillboxes will spot us."

"Okay, when I give the word, bounce for that bridge. Set your Y-racks on automatic. They'll drop grenades behind you as you come. Don't move out until I tell you. Miller?"

"I'm all right, Julian."

Now that action is imminent, Miller seems calmed down, Julian thought. He checked his own rocket launcher and hand flamer, then readied some fire pills.

"LeClerc. Ready?"

"Ready, Julian."

"You and I bounce on my signal."

Julian poked his head above the rise. He could clearly see the road in front of him and the two Skinny pillboxes facing him. Across the bridge, flames were devouring a section of the city. There was nothing else to see. Julian knew he'd spot the pillboxes on the other side at the top of his bounce. For an instant, he wondered if any of the Skinny civilians who had run from the park were watching, or maybe alerting that Skinny patrol. No time to worry now.

"LeClerc, *bounce!*"

Julian leapt skyward and forward. He squeezed the first trigger on his rocket launcher at the top of his bounce. The rocket spotted the rear of the left pillbox across the river and locked on target. Julian squeezed the second trigger, and the rocket leapt toward its target as he descended near the left pillbox on his own side of the river.

"Now, squad! Move, move, *move!* On the bounce!"

Woczinski, Miller, and Estrada leapt from their hiding places, grenades from their Y-racks arcing behind them. Then disaster hit the squad. From far to the east, another air-defense gun opened fire, aiming straight down the bridge! At the same time, the west-bank pillboxes opened up on the bouncing men. Julian barely had time to realize what had happened. The Skinnies across the river had seen Woczinski's group moving up, radioed for fire support from an east-bank gun, and waited for the M.I. to make their move!

There are a total of twenty-two Skinnies firing at Julian's squad: sixteen in the pillboxes and six manning the east-side air-defense gun. Each Skinny has an Ordnance value of 4 rather than the usual 3. This reflects the higher firepower of the gun.

The Skinnies fire using Chart D.

Julian's squad fires using Chart E.

The combat lasts for only four rounds, then the Skinnies withdraw.

If any squad members besides Julian are alive at the end of the combat, go to section 46.

If Julian is the only M.I. survivor, go to section 43.

If the squad is wiped out, go to section 48.

— 48 —

There's thirty seconds I'll never forget, Julian thought as he lay panting in the dirt.

The Skinnies had been surprised, but they caught on real quick. They were firing by the time Julian gave the order for Woczinski, Miller, and Estrada to rush across the bridge. It seemed to Julian as though everything had happened in slow motion. He could still see his three men emerging from the smoke in the middle of the bridge, bouncing high. He could see the laser fire directed at him from the east-side pillboxes. The grenade explosions were almost deafening. The Skinnies in the pillboxes had grenade launchers, and their ordnance added to the din of the bombs tossed from the M.I.'s Y-racks.

The Skinnies on the west side of the bridge were no dopes either. As soon as Woczinski and company had made their dash, those Skinnies darted out of their pillbox, swinging one of their pulse lasers around with them. That thing had sent a stream of laser fire right down the length of the bridge. And the Skinnies firing the thing were good. Julian saw them cut down Miller and Estrada. Then a grenade from one of the east-side pillboxes knocked out LeClerc. Woczinski died not five yards from Julian. Just as he unleashed another rocket, a searing pain sent Julian into darkness as well.

Go to section 29.

— **49** —

"We move north, parallel to the river, exactly as in the original plan," Julian announced. "Alternate bounces; use those low industrial buildings for cover on the ground. We'll advance in a rough line running east to west—don't drag up the rear. I'll take the right flank position. Be sure to set your Y-rack on automatic. We want to do as much damage as possible to those Skinny industrial facilities."

One good bounce, and each man was away from the carnage by the bridge. They proceeded north with relative safety. Air-defense gunners need time to track their target for accurate fire, and a bouncing M.I. isn't in the air long enough to become a good target.

"I can see the waterworks," Woczinski sang out. "How about a few little presents for our pretend target?"

"By all means—good idea," Julian concurred.

Explosions soon rocked the waterworks area. From the top of his next bounce, Julian saw Skinny civilians fleeing the works buildings. Better yet, he also spotted that Skinny patrol. It was moving into a defensive position, taking the bait and attempting to block the M.I.'s progress toward the water plant.

"Great shooting, Woczinski! Keep it up—the feint is working. Let's see if we can hit that air-defense gun position just east of the waterworks as well."

The advance continued until they reached a point about a hundred yards south of the east-west highway near the waterworks. Then Julian ordered the swing.

"Okay, turn now. I'll still be on the right flank. We'll arc back and come in on the target area from the west-southwest."

As they executed their turn, Julian surveyed the ground already covered. Excellent, he thought. Flames from the warehouse area were already spreading to the urban center. The industrial areas they'd passed through were a burning shambles, with occasional secondary explosions as volatile chemicals went up. Civilians, for the most part, were fleeing north, away from the real target area. Whoever drew up this plan knew their stuff, Julian thought.

And I'd better think up a plan of attack on our target. There are two ways to do it. The streets below are clearing. We could go to ground about two hundred yards from the target, sneak up, and attempt to attack by surprise. Or, we could keep bouncing and bounce our way right into the compound. If we do that, the guards in those towers just might think we're only passing through. They might not realize their precious secret think-tank is the real target of this raid.

Look at Map 2. It shows the Skinny defenses in the R&D facility compound. (Map 2 is in section 15.)

If Julian orders the squad to go to ground and move up under cover for a sneak attack, go to section 92.

*If Julian chooses to rush the compound "on the bounce,"
go to section 93.*

— 50 —

"We'll save some time and go straight for the target,"
Julian ordered. "Move out, on the bounce. Use the industrial buildings for cover, set Y-rack on automatic. We'll
advance in a rough line; don't drag up the rear. Alternate
bounces to keep the enemy guessing."

At the top of his first bounce, Julian realized he could
see the waterworks.

"Fire some rockets at the waterworks. We may or may
not do some damage, but it could make the Skinnies think
that's the real target," Julian ordered.

He noticed with pleasure that the Y-rack bombs were
already doing their job: blowing through the rooftops of
industrial buildings, causing panic, starting fires.

Bouncing through the industrial area was relatively easy
work. The air-defense gunners needed precious seconds to
track and train their pieces on a target, and bouncing M.I.
don't stay in the air long enough to make good targets. The
terrain was flat, and the Skinny buildings were long, low
structures. Lots of open terrain—parking and loading
facilities—alternating with an assortment of odd-shaped
buildings. Just like an industrial park back on Terra, Julian
mused.

Distant explosions rocked the waterworks.

"Nice shooting, Woczinski," Julian called.

Julian headed north and east. As the men alternated
bounces over an east-west major roadway, Julian spotted
the target building. Just as in the briefing: four guard
towers behind a high wire fence, big parking and loading

area, an L-shaped building. That's where the Skinny planners were located.

Two plans of attack formed in Julian's mind. He could go to ground around the southwest corner of the building, try to sneak up on those towers, and then hit with the advantage of surprise. Or, he could use the good range of the rocket launchers to take out the towers as they bounced in. Possibly the Skinnies would think they were on a typical raid and expect them to bounce right past, never thinking that their secret think-tank was the real target.

Look at Map 2. It shows the Skinny defenses in the target R&D complex as they appear to Julian.

If Julian orders the squad to go to ground, attempting to sneak up on the target complex, go to section 90.

If Julian orders the squad to bounce right into the place, go to section 91.

— 51 —

There's a minute of time I'll never forget as long as I live, Julian mused while reloading his rocket launcher and checking the go-juice and jump-juice readouts on his powered armor.

It all seemed to happen in slow motion. First, the explosions from the covering rocket fire. The rush toward the pillbox. The laser fire seeming to come from everywhere. The hand bombs exploding. Dust, smoke, screams, and death. The Skinnies in the two remaining pillboxes hadn't waited to be rooted out; they'd come out firing to retake the structures lost by their comrades. Instead of an orderly tactical exercise, the thing had turned into a chaotic turmoil of fear and death.

But now it's over, Julian thought grimly. And we won . . . sort of. I guess you could call this winning. Doesn't matter, though. That Skinny patrol is somewhere around. Less than fifteen minutes left to accomplish our mission.

"Where to, Julian?"

The voice let Julian know Woczinski was not only still alive, but in good shape, ready for more action. Wish I felt so enthusiastic, Julian thought.

"Just a sec. I'm planning. Check out your weapons and equipment and prepare to move out."

Two options, Julian thought. Stick to the plan and head north along the east bank of the river. That's the feint, just might draw off that patrol. But time's rushing by. Much faster to move directly toward the target. Which option is better? Have to decide, and decide fast.

Be sure to record losses to the squad. Deduct 1 point from the squad's Morale value for each man killed. Add 1 point to Morale for winning the fight.

If Julian decides to continue north along the east side of the river, following the original plan, go to section 49.

If Julian decides to head directly for the target site, go to section 50.

— 52 —

To Julian, time seemed to slow to a crawl. His neat, clean tactical plan had turned into a smoking chaos of explosive noise, flashing laser fire, searing pain, and death, all in slow motion.

The pillboxes on the west side cut down the rookies Miller and Estrada as soon as they moved out. Woczinski went down, but didn't die right away. Julian was bouncing over the middle of the bridge and had managed to flame one Skinny who was headed toward Woczinski to administer the coup de grace.

Julian never knew how LeClerc bought his farm. He was too busy to see it happen. The last thing he knew, a Skinny had manhandled one of the pulse lasers out of a pillbox and was aiming it down the bridge. Julian slapped another rocket into his launcher. It was the last thing he did.

Go to section 29.

— 53 —

"Squad, proceed north past Bridge Two, using buildings for cover from pillbox fire. The Skinnies in the pillboxes at Bridge One came out to follow us after we went past them. If the ones at Bridge Two are so obliging, we'll double back on them. Then LeClerc and I will lay down covering fire while Woczinski, Miller, and Estrada rush across to the east side. With those pillboxes undermanned, we have a good chance to pull this off," Julian ordered, then clicked off his squad circuit.

"I hope," Julian added in a whisper to himself alone.

Two bounces later, Julian saw he'd made the right decision. Sure enough, as the squad passed, two Skinnies from each of the four pillboxes at Bridge Two rushed outside. They jumped into vehicles and began proceeding north, one vehicle on each side of the river, following the bouncing M.I. troopers. Far ahead, Julian saw the Skinny patrol deploying into defensive positions around the waterworks.

Julian waited until his squad was in a rough east-to-west line about three hundred yards north of Bridge Two.

"Now, squad, turn in toward the river and stay down after your next bounce. Use fire pills to clear the street ahead of you and make for the bridge. Woczinski, Miller, Estrada: take cover within rushing distance of your end of the bridge. LeClerc, follow me and raise all the cain you can. When we get near the bridge, use your rockets on those pillboxes. They won't do much good, but they'll kick up a ton of debris and dust. Might give the others some cover when they cross."

Roll two dice. If the result is the same as or less than the squad's Stealth value, go to section 55.

If the result of the roll is greater than the squad's Stealth value, go to section 57.

— 54 —

"We don't take the bridge. That's a waste of time," Julian snapped. "But we do rush the pillboxes. Turn in toward the bridge now. As you approach, go to cover and advance with stealth. We'll do the same over here. When you're set, LeClerc and I will lay down covering fire, and bounce around a bit to draw the Skinny fire. Then Estrada, Miller, and Woczinski, you rush across. Got it?"

When a combat officer asks a question in the middle of a firefight, he expects an answer. Julian listened to the silence, which lasted . . . and lasted . . . and lasted as precious seconds ticked by.

They aren't answering, Julian thought. They aren't answering for some very good reason.

On the west side of the river, Miller, Estrada, and Woczinski thought about the forty-yard-wide bridge and about the more than 150 yards they would have to run.

They thought about all that open area; a perfect killing ground for gunners in those pillboxes. They thought about the kind of leader they'd heard Julian was.

Roll two dice. If the result is the same as or less than the squad's Morale value, go to section 56.

If the result of the roll is greater than the squad's Morale value, go to section 58.

— 55 —

Julian dropped some fire pills into the street below, and watched a crowd of civilian Skinnies scatter as they landed.

"Now LeClerc, come on down. The streets are fine."

"But of course, *mon capitaine*," LeClerc responded.

The two men cut southwest at a dead run through the flaming industrial center. The Y-racks on their backs spewed enough grenades to keep any curious civilians from following them closely.

Now, thought Julian, if only the Skinnies don't spot us or Woczinski and company approaching the bridge, we'll be in business.

Julian reached the steep grade leading up to the major highway, which paralleled the river. He hurled himself prone near the top of the rise. LeClerc was to his left, about fifty yards away. Traffic on the highway had come to a dead stop. The Skinnies had abandoned their vehicles and fled for cover.

Just over the rise, Julian saw the two Skinny pillboxes on his side of the river.

"It's working, men. I can see one of those Skinny troopers coming out of the pillbox to look around."

"So far, so good on our side," came Woczinski's reply.

"We're about fifteen yards from the end of the bridge, so close to those Skinny pillboxes we could smell them. We have good cover here from the burning buildings. Lots of smoke. I don't think those Skinnies have infrared."

Julian took a final quick look toward the pillboxes, checked the length of the bridge toward the flaming buildings in the urban center, then ducked back down out of sight.

"Here we go. Everyone, fire one rocket at a pillbox on the west side. LeClerc, you and I will bounce on 'one,' and fire. On 'two,' Woczinski, Miller, and Estrada fire, then bounce. With any luck, the Skinnies still in the pillboxes here on the east side will fire at me and LeClerc, so keep your bounce low, Frenchie, and get down fast.

"Okay, by the numbers! One!"

Julian pushed himself into the air, fired a rocket at the rear of one of the west-bank pillboxes, and dove back toward the cover of the highway embankment. The Skinny outside the pillbox was too stunned even to move. Julian saw LeClerc hit the dirt nearby, then heard the explosions of the rockets.

"Two!"

Three rockets leapt toward the same targets, this time from the west, and three M.I. troopers were in the air, bouncing down a third of the length of Bridge Two. The structure was a good forty yards wide. No danger of missing and landing in the drink.

But by the time Miller, Estrada, and Woczinski were in the air, the startled Skinnies had recovered enough to return fire using their laser gun.

There are a total of eight Skinnies (two per pillbox) with an Ordnance value of 3 each.

The Skinnies fire using Chart E.

Julian's squad fires using Chart C.

Combat continues until Julian's squad is wiped out, all the Skinnies are wiped out, or the end of four complete rounds.

If Julian is the sole M.I. survivor, go to section 60.

If Julian and at least one other M.I. survive, go to section 59.

If the squad is completely wiped out, go to section 62.

— 56 —

Estrada's voice broke the silence.

"Hey man, sure, you know what to do, we do it! Come on, guys, we're the M.I., not a bunch of civilian trainees on parade!"

"Okay, Julian, you got it. Let's go over it once more."

Certainly, Woczinski, Julian thought to himself. I've got nothing better to do at the moment. But Julian knew he couldn't allow that sarcasm to show in his voice when he ordered, "Squad, turn in toward the bridge, now! At two hundred yards, go to cover in the streets. Use fire pills to clear out civilians. Approach the bridge as closely as possible without being seen. Everyone contact me when you're in position. LeClerc, flank me on the left. Let's move!"

Two hundred yards from the bridge, Julian dropped some fire pills into the street below, then watched a crowd of civilian Skinnies scatter as he landed.

"Now LeClerc, come on down. The streets are fine."

"*Mais oui, mon capitaine,*" LeClerc responded.

The two men cut northwest at a dead run through the flaming industrial center. The Y-racks on their backs spewed enough grenades to keep any curious civilians from following them too closely.

Now, thought Julian, if only the Skinnies don't spot us or Woczinski and company approaching the bridge, we'll be in business.

Roll two dice. If the result is the same as or less than the squad's Stealth value, go to section 64.

If the result of the roll is greater than the squad's Stealth value, go to section 65.

— 57 —

Julian dropped some fire pills into the street below, then watched a crowd of civilian Skinnies scatter as he landed.

"Now LeClerc, come on down. The streets are fine."

"*Mais oui, mon capitaine,*" LeClerc responded.

The two men cut southwest at a dead run through the flaming industrial center. The Y-racks on their backs spewed enough grenades to keep any curious civilians from following them too closely.

Now, thought Julian, if only the Skinnies don't spot us or Woczinski and company approaching the bridge, we'll be in business.

Julian reached the steep grade leading up to the major highway, which paralleled the river. He hurled himself prone near the top of the rise. LeClerc was to his left, about fifty yards away. Traffic on the highway had come to a dead stop. The Skinnies had abandoned their vehicles and fled for cover.

Just over the rise, Julian saw the two Skinny pillboxes on his side of the river.

"It's working, men. I can see one of those Skinny troopers coming out of the pillbox to look around."

"So far, so good on our side," came Woczinski's reply.

"We're about fifteen yards from the end of the bridge, so close to those Skinny pillboxes we could smell them. We have good cover here from the burning buildings. Lots of smoke. I don't think those Skinnies have infrared."

Julian took a final quick look toward the pillboxes, checked the length of the bridge toward the flaming buildings in the urban center, then ducked back down out of sight.

"Here we go. Everyone, fire one rocket at a pillbox on the west side. LeClerc, you and I will bounce on 'one,' and fire. On 'two,' Woczinski, Miller, and Estrada fire, then bounce. With any luck, the Skinnies still in the pillboxes here on the east side will fire at me and LeClerc, so keep your bounce low, Frenchie, and get down fast.

"Okay, by the numbers! One!"

Julian pushed himself into the air and let his rocket see its target. Suddenly, a chaos of laser fire and grenades broke loose all around him. He managed to squeeze the trigger, launching the rocket, and hit the dirt again.

No good! There was Skinny fire coming from behind him, too!

"They're everywhere!" LeClerc called. "Must have seen us approach—those Skinnies who were in their vehicles followed us as we doubled back!"

There are a total of sixteen Skinnies (two each in four pillboxes and four each in two vehicles) with an Ordnance value of 3 each.

The Skinnies fire using Chart D.

Julian's squad fires using Chart C.

Combat continues until Julian's squad is wiped out or all the Skinnies are wiped out.

If Julian is the sole M.I. survivor, go to section 60.

If Julian and at least one other M.I. survive the fight, go to section 59.

If the squad is completely wiped out, go to section 62.

— 58 —

"We've been talking it over, Julian," Woczinski's voice came over the comm unit, "and we don't think rushing that open bridge is such a good idea. Frankly, we don't think there's any chance at all of making it."

Julian's mind reeled. Not again! Just like Paolo, only worse. This amounts to outright mutiny in the field. Well, almost. But, is this the time to press the matter? If my authority breaks down now, we'll all die, probably within minutes. Okay, we're expendable, but I'd like to stay alive. Or at least I'd like to accomplish something if I have to die.

Maybe I'm overreacting. Maybe they just need encouragement. They haven't flat refused to obey—yet. Got to reestablish authority.

"Listen up, you apes! Since when do M.I. 'talk over' their orders in the middle of a combat mission? There will be no dissent. In combat, dissent leads to division and division leads to disaster. You're on the verge of mutiny, which means you'll die whether or not you get off this Skinny-infested rock. Obey now and I'll forget this. Answer!"

Again, silence.

Roll two dice. If the result is the same as or less than the squad's Morale value, go to section 56.

If the result of the roll is greater than the squad's Morale value, go to section 61.

— 59 —

Combat is exhilarating, exhausting, and sickening. Skinnies, despite their eight-foot height, low body weight, and natural disdain for clothing, look at least slightly human. They have heads, hands, feet, feelings, and families.

"Don't let it get to you, Julian. You're in command. What next?"

The voice was soft, low pitched, firm.

"Thanks, Woczinski. I guess it doesn't matter much if any of that Skinny mess out there had a Skinny babe waiting at home, does it? Never mind.

"We've wasted valuable time here. We've been on the ground four minutes. The Skinny patrol is deploying around their waterworks, right where we want it—at least, they were, until this firefight. We'll head straight for the target. Alternate bounces, move on the ground between bounces. Cease firing now. We've set enough fires to keep them busy. New firing will just give away our general direction of advance."

Be sure to mark off any casualties suffered by the squad in the fight at Bridge Two. Deduct 1 from the squad's Morale value for each casualty suffered, then add 1 for overcoming the Skinny resistance. Go to section 67.

— 60 —

At first, it looked as though the M.I. had a chance. But things went sour quickly.

Julian saw it all—it happened fast, but it seemed to take forever.

First, he saw Skinny laser fire take down Miller. The short-range fire cut through the man's powered armor, man and suit went down, and Julian heard the stifled scream over his comm unit.

Grenades took out Woczinski and Estrada. They were too close together, landing from a bounce at the same time within five yards of each other. No good. A grenade landed between them. The Skinny with the grenade launcher knew a good thing when he saw it; he pumped four more into the same area, quickly. Two more farms, bought and paid for.

Julian almost managed to save LeClerc. His rocket took out a Skinny pulse laser just a second too late.

Julian survived the carnage for only a few seconds. Then he ran. He didn't know where, in particular; he just ran. Skinny patrols were out in force after the firefight at Bridge Two, of course. Eventually he ran into one, and Julian Penn's war was over.

Go to section 29.

— 61 —

Julian never got his answer.

At least, not in words.

He got his answer from the actions of his men, and it wasn't the answer he wanted.

The silent waiting was broken when Julian saw Woczinski bouncing away to the northwest. He was followed by Estrada and, finally, by Miller.

"What's with those guys, LeClerc?"

"Beats me. Want to try to make it to the retrieval point?"

"Right. We'll stick with the mission. Alternate bounces and move out to the northeast toward the target."

"Sure. You go first."

Julian heard it in LeClerc's voice.

One man alone never had a chance against the guard towers at the target. Julian learned that by trying.

Go to section 29.

— 62 —

At first, it looked as though the M.I. had a chance. But things went sour quickly.

Julian saw it all—it happened fast, but it seemed to take forever.

First, he saw Skinny laser fire take down Miller. The short-range fire cut through the man's powered armor, man and suit went down, and Julian heard the stifled scream over his comm unit.

Grenades took out Woczinski and Estrada. They were too close together, landing from a bounce at the same time within five yards of each other. No good. A grenade landed between them. The Skinny with the grenade launcher knew a good thing when he saw it; he pumped four more into the same area, quickly. Two more farms, bought and paid for.

Julian almost managed to save LeClerc. His rocket took out a Skinny pulse laser just a second too late. He knew he was about to take out a mortgage himself when a grenade blast knocked him over.

Just like Woczinski, Julian thought. If I can just get up in time . . .

It was the last thing he ever wanted to do.

Go to section 29.

— 63 —

The M.I. opened fire at the same time as the Skinnies. There were lots and lots of Skinnies, and every time Julian bounced, he saw more on the way. Somehow, they must have known what to expect, he thought.

At the top of his next bounce, Julian fired a rocket toward a Skinny jeep making its way across Bridge One.

No, they didn't know what to expect, Julian muttered to himself. They figured it out because I messed up. Should have bounced. Time, time, time. That's the vital thing in a raid like this. I wasted time, and it's probably going to cost me this squad.

Julian bounced again, saw flames rising from the warehouse district, saw Woczinski flame down three Skinny troopers, saw Miller cut in half by laser fire.

"Miller's down," Woczinski reported.

"Don't attempt pickup now. Keep firing."

Yeah. We'll keep firing. Only thing to do. At least we can die with some honor, despite my stupidity.

Julian was the last of the squad to die. He went down proud of his troops, less proud of his ability to command.

Go to section 29.

— 64 —

Julian reached the steep grade leading up to the major highway, which paralleled the river. He hurled himself prone near the top of the rise. LeClerc was to his left, about fifty yards away. Traffic on the highway had come to a dead stop. The Skinnies had abandoned their vehicles and fled for cover.

Just over the rise, Julian saw the two Skinny pillboxes on his side of the river.

"It's working, men. I can see one of those Skinny troopers coming out of the pillbox to look around."

"So far, so good on our side," came Woczinski's reply. "We're about fifteen yards from the end of the bridge, so close to those Skinny pillboxes we could smell them. We have good cover here from the burning buildings. Lots of smoke. I don't think those Skinnies have infrared."

Julian took a final quick look toward the pillboxes, checked the length of the bridge toward the flaming buildings in the urban center, then ducked back down out of sight.

"Here we go. Everyone, fire one rocket at a pillbox on the west side. LeClerc, you and I will bounce on 'one,' and fire. On 'two,' Woczinski, Miller, and Estrada fire, then bounce. With any luck, the Skinnies still in the pillboxes here on the east side will fire at me and LeClerc, so keep your bounce low, Frenchie, and get down fast.

"Okay, by the numbers! One!"

Julian pushed himself into the air and fired a rocket at the rear of one of the west-bank pillboxes, then dove back toward the cover of the highway embankment. The Skinny outside the pillbox was too stunned to even move. Julian saw LeClerc hit the dirt nearby, then heard the explosions of the rockets.

"Two!"

Three rockets leapt toward the same targets, this time from the west, and three M.I. troopers were in the air, bouncing down a third of the length of Bridge Two. The structure was a good forty yards wide. No danger of missing and landing in the drink.

But by the time Miller, Estrada, and Woczinski were in the air, the startled Skinnies had recovered enough to return fire using their laser guns.

There are a total of sixteen Skinnies (four per pillbox) with an Ordnance value of 3 each.

The Skinnies fire using Chart E.

Julian's squad fires using Chart C.

Combat continues until Julian's squad is wiped out, all the Skinnies are killed, or the end of four complete rounds.

If Julian is the sole M.I. survivor, go to section 60.

If Julian and at least one other M.I. survive, go to section 59.

If the squad is completely wiped out, go to section 62.

— 65 —

Julian reached the steep grade leading up to the major highway, which paralleled the river. He hurled himself prone near the top of the rise. LeClerc was to his left, about fifty yards away. Traffic on the highway had come to a dead stop. The Skinnies had abandoned their vehicles and fled for cover.

Just over the rise, Julian saw the two Skinny pillboxes on his side of the river.

"It's working, men. I can see one of those Skinny troopers coming out of the pillbox to look around."

"So far, so good on our side," came Woczinski's reply. "We're about fifteen yards from the end of the bridge, so close to those Skinny pillboxes we could smell them. We have good cover here from the burning buildings. Lots of smoke. I don't think those Skinnies have infrared."

Julian took a final quick look toward the pillboxes, checked the length of the bridge toward the flaming buildings in the urban center, then ducked back down out of sight.

"Here we go. Everyone, fire one rocket at a pillbox on the west side. LeClerc, you and I will bounce on 'one,' and fire. On 'two,' Woczinski, Miller, and Estrada fire, then bounce. With any luck, the Skinnies still in the pillboxes here on the east side will fire at me and LeClerc, so keep your bounce low, Frenchie, and get down fast.

"Okay, by the numbers! One!"

Julian pushed himself into the air and let his rocket see its target. Suddenly, a chaos of laser fire and grenades broke loose all around him. He managed to squeeze the trigger, launching the rocket, and hit the dirt again.

No good! There was Skinny fire coming from behind him, too!

"They're everywhere!" LeClerc called. "Must have seen us approach—those Skinnies from Bridge One who were in their vehicles followed us somehow."

There are a total of twenty-four Skinnies (four each in four pillboxes and four each in two vehicles) with an Ordnance value of 3 each.

The Skinnies fire using Chart D.

Julian's squad fires using Chart C.

Combat continues until Julian's squad is wiped out or all the Skinnies are wiped out.

If Julian is the sole M.I. survivor, go to section 60.

If Julian and at least one other M.I. survive, go to section 59.

If the squad is completely wiped out, go to section 62.

— 66 —

"Skinnies! Skinnies everywhere!"

Miller's scream of panic infected the whole squad. It was true, Julian saw. There were Skinnies everywhere. The slow progress of the M.I., their failure to spread confusion and destruction as part of a rapid advance, allowed the Skinny command structure sufficient time to respond. Civilian guardsmen, trained to watch for patterns in M.I. raids and radio them to regular troops, alerted the patrol to the precise locations of Julian's troopers.

The squad broke just seconds after Miller panicked. Julian had time to learn two vital lessons. One, speed in a raid is essential, no matter what the danger from enemy firepower. Two, panic is contagious, perhaps more contagious than valor. Green troops poorly led will break quickly.

Unfortunately, Julian never had time to make use of these two hard-won lessons. The Skinny regulars had no trouble mopping up. Julian went down fighting, still calling commands, attempting to rally his broken men.

Go to section 29.

— 67 —

The squad moved out on the bounce, heading east-northeast toward the Skinny R&D facility. Julian picked a route that got them quickly away from the major highway.

The advance was relatively safe. Bouncing M.I. troopers make poor targets for air-defense gunners. The troopers don't stay aloft long enough for the gunners to track them and aim their weapons well.

Julian noticed that despite the foul-ups, the overall plan seemed to be working. His troops were sowing havoc in the industrial sector. Their Y-rack bombs were starting lots of fires, and most of the civilians not under cover were fleeing north, away from the intended target area. Whoever dreamed up this plan knew something, Julian thought.

And speaking of dreaming up plans, I'd better come up with one for the attack on this compound. Two ways to do it. We could go to ground about two hundred yards from the target, move down there among those factories, and sneak into good positions. Then we could hit them all at once with the benefit of surprise. Or, we could just keep bouncing right toward them. The Skinnies in those towers will probably assume it's just the pattern of our raid that brings us their way and limit themselves to sporadic potshots. One bounce later, we'll be right in with them.

Either way could work—what do I order?

Look at Map 2, which shows the Skinny defenses around the R&D facility.

If Julian orders the squad to go to ground and move into position for a sneak attack, go to section 92.

If Julian decides to attack the compound "on the bounce," go to Section 93.

— **68** —

"Squad, go to ground! We'll make the Skinnies look for us the hard way. Keep advancing in a northeasterly direction, but stay in the streets, don't bounce, and use the buildings for cover. Use rockets and Y-rack bombs to cause structure damage and get some fires going."

Julian called the order from the top of his last bounce. He saw Woczinski hit the street, toss an incendiary into a factory window, and dash north. Julian armed a rocket, readied his hand flamer, set his Y-rack on automatic, and hit a minor street about a block north of Woczinski.

Mistake! Julian's Y-rack was tossing bombs directly behind Julian, right into Woczinski's path of advance. And a Skinny dead ahead was hiding around a building corner, taking potshots.

Julian dove for cover, flipped on his tactical display, and called, "Woczinski! Back out of there. Swing around to my right. Form a line with me as the left flanker!"

Julian rolled into a doorway as a grenade landed in the street thirty feet in front of him.

The Skinny patrol is attacking in force and with tactical precision. This is their territory. They know the buildings and the street layout. The patrol consists of sixteen Skinnies, each with an Ordnance value of 3.

The Skinnies fire using Chart D.

Julian's squad fires using Chart E.

The combat continues until either all the Skinnies are killed or all the M.I. are killed.

If all the Skinnies are killed, and Julian is the sole M.I. survivor, go to section 74.

If all the Skinnies are killed, and at least one M.I. in addition to Julian survives the fight, go to section 70.

If all the M.I. are killed, go to section 71.

— 69 —

"Belay that order about not firing forward. Blast anything that looks dangerous or even promising, except the real target building itself. Advance on the bounce, by the numbers. We'll deal with that patrol as we close on the target. Bounce right over the fence, take out the guard towers as you glide over. Then make for the west doors of the R&D building.

"We'll converge toward the southwest corner of the complex as we advance, and enter over the south and west sides of their fence."

Julian bounced as he gave his orders, firing a rocket at one of the Skinny jeeps. Best way to lead is by example, he said to himself.

There are a total of sixteen Skinnies in the patrol. Each Skinny has an Ordnance value of 3.

The M.I. fire using Chart C.

The Skinnies fire using Chart F.

Fight three rounds of combat. At the end of three rounds, the M.I. have passed the patrol's position and are closing on the real target of their raid. This firefight ends after 3 rounds of combat.

If two or more M.I. survive, go to section 85.

If Julian is the sole M.I. survivor, go to section 86.

If no M.I. survive, go to section 87.

— 70 —

Julian never knew how the squad managed to do it.

Skinny laser fire and grenades seemed to leap from everywhere. The flaming factories and the thick, black, acrid smoke helped the Skinnies as much as it helped the M.I. The M.I. powered armor equipped with infrared snoopers usually gave a great edge over Skinnies. Their body temperature is high, and they glow like neon signs in infrared. But, in the midst of industrial fires where infrared was next to useless, in terrain they knew like the backs of their elongated hands, the Skinnies were formidable.

Julian fired, rolled, stood up, advanced, checked his tactical display, and kept the squad bearing northeast toward the target. Then he did it again. And again. And again.

He turned a corner, and flamed one Skinny at point-blank range. Hopping over the flaming body, he dove through a window to avoid a grenade, slammed a rocket into a passing Skinny jeep, and paused for two seconds to check his tactical display.

"Woczinski, report; I can't see you."

"I'm down too low; found an underground tunnel connecting two buildings. Uh-oh!" The sudden silence from Woczinski was ominous.

"I'm back," Woczinski reported. "The Skinnies knew about the tunnel, too." Julian breathed a sigh of relief.

It went on for a long, long time, and then it stopped suddenly. Julian lay quietly, hand flamer ready. It took him half a minute to realize there was no hostile fire.

"Squad, report, by the numbers."

Julian waited for the reports, then counted his men.

The trembling started then. Julian lay in the rubble of a burning building and shook. He lost track of time until the music that signaled recall brought him around.

The beacon! Time's up! Three minutes to get to the retrieval boat!

"Beacon, Julian. And the target's just ahead."

Good old Woczinski. Doesn't anything rattle him? Julian wondered. Now, we've only got three minutes.

"You have the target on visual?"

"Affirmative. Outer fence one hundred yards away."

If Julian gives the order to lay low, then make for the retrieval point exactly in time to catch the retrieval boat, go to section 72.

If Julian decides to attempt the raid on the target building and take prisoners before the boat arrives, go to section 73.

— 71 —

Julian never knew the squad was wiped out.

Skinny laser fire and grenades seemed to leap from everywhere. The flaming factories and the thick, black, acrid smoke helped the Skinnies as much as it helped the M.I. The M.I. powered armor equipped with infrared snoopers usually gave a great edge over Skinnies. Their body temperature is high, and they glow like neon signs in infrared. But, in the midst of industrial fires where infrared was next to useless, in terrain they knew like the backs of their elongated hands, the Skinnies were formidable.

Julian fired, rolled, stood up, advanced, checked his tactical display, and kept the squad bearing northeast toward the target. Then he did it again. And again. And again.

He turned a corner and flamed one Skinny at point-blank range. Hopping over the flaming body, he dove through a window to avoid a grenade, slammed a rocket into a passing Skinny jeep, and paused for two seconds to check his tactical display.

"Woczinski, report; I can't see you."

"I'm down too low; found an underground tunnel connecting two buildings. Uh-oh!" The sudden silence from Woczinski was ominous.

"I'm back," Woczinski reported. "The Skinnies knew about the tunnel, too." Julian breathed a sigh of relief.

It went on for a long, long time, and then it stopped suddenly. Julian lay quietly, hand flamer ready. It took him half a minute to realize there was no hostile fire.

"Squad, report, by the numbers."

Julian waited for the reports, then counted his dead.

The trembling started then. Julian lay in the rubble of a burning building and shook. He lost track of time until the music that signaled recall brought him around.

The beacon! Time's up! Three minutes to get to the retrieval boat!

Julian staggered to his feet, made a quick visual check up and down the street, and bounced out of the rubble. He never saw the Skinny, the one with the laser rifle, who cut him down.

Go to section 29.

— 72 —

"All right. We'll lay low until fifteen seconds before the boat lands. By then we should have it on visual. Then, on my signal, we bounce once, take out the guard towers, bounce again, take out any remaining guards, land right on the retrieval point and board. Got it?"

"Sure."

Well, I know the sound of disgust when I hear it, Julian thought. Hell, I'm disgusted too. To have come all this way and then not have time to carry out the mission is galling. But the M.I. take care of their own, and I intend to bring our survivors back alive.

"Okay, let's move up to within fifty yards. Stay down and don't let them see you."

Julian crossed a street, flattened against a building, and peered around the corner. He could just make out the guard tower at the southwest corner of the target compound. The guards were watching the flaming inferno in the industrial area. Julian advanced, ducking into doorways and peeking out before moving on. He had worked his way to within fifty yards of the fence when his tactical display showed the squad was in position. Then came the waiting.

Roll two dice. If the result is the same as or less than the squad's Stealth value, go to section 75.

If the result of the roll is greater than the squad's Stealth value, go to section 76.

— 73 —

"We came here to do a job, and the M.I. have a tradition of getting the job done. We're going to do it. We're going to go in there, grab some prisoners, and then make that retrieval boat."

"Good."

Glad to hear it, Woczinski, Julian thought. After all the other fiascoes so far on this drop, glad to hear you don't want to just cut and run.

"First thing to do is work our way up to the target

compound without being seen. We'll make for a spot about fifty yards from the southwest corner. Then we'll bounce together over the fence, taking out one guard tower each as we go. We can get the rest of the towers from the ground. Then we'll hit the doors at the west end of the building.''

"Got it."

"Okay, M.I., let's move!''

Julian crossed a street, flattened against a building, and peered around the corner. He could just make out the guard tower at the southwest corner of the target compound. The guards were watching the flaming inferno in the industrial area. Julian advanced, ducking into doorways, and peeking out before advancing again. He had worked his way to within fifty yards of the fence when his tactical display showed the squad was in position.

Roll two dice. If the result is the same as or less than the squad's Stealth value, go to section 80.

If the result is greater than the squad's Stealth value, go to section 81.

— 74 —

Julian couldn't figure out how he was still alive.

Skinny laser fire and grenades seemed to leap from everywhere. The flaming factories and the thick, black, acrid smoke helped the Skinnies as much as it helped the M.I. The M.I. powered armor equipped with infrared snoopers usually gave a great edge over Skinnies. Their body temperature is high, and they glow like neon signs in infrared. But, in the midst of industrial fires where infrared was next to useless, in terrain they knew like the backs of their elongated hands, the Skinnies were formidable.

Julian fired, rolled, stood up, advanced, checked his tactical display, and kept the squad bearing northeast toward the target. Then he did it again. And again. And again.

He turned a corner and flamed one Skinny at point-blank range. Hopping over the flaming body, he dove through a window to avoid a grenade, slammed a rocket into a passing Skinny jeep, and paused for two seconds to check his tactical display.

"Woczinski, report; I can't see you."

"I'm down too low; found an underground tunnel connecting two buildings. Uh-oh!" The sudden silence from Woczinski was ominous.

"I'm back," Woczinski reported. "The Skinnies knew about the tunnel, too."

It went on for a long, long time, and then it stopped suddenly. Julian lay quietly, hand flamer ready. It took him half a minute to realize there was no hostile fire.

"Squad, report, by the numbers."

Julian waited for the reports. There were none.

The trembling started then. Julian lay in the rubble of a burning building and shook. He lost track of time until the music that signaled recall brought him around.

The beacon! Time's up! Three minutes to get to the retrieval boat! Guess I'll give it that old M.I. try.

Julian struggled to his feet, staggered northeast across a minor street, tossed a bomb into the factory to his right, then staggered forward another fifty yards. He saw the wire fence around the target building. Guards in towers at the corners manned heavy weapons.

One bounce, and Julian sent a rocket hurtling toward one tower while he used the hand flamer on the guards in another while sailing over the fence.

Two towers left, thought Julian. I'll never make it.

His last thought was correct. The remaining guards cut him down before he hit the ground.

Go to section 29.

— 75 —

Julian first saw the boat as a tiny pinpoint of flame high in the sky. The sound followed in a few seconds. Better move before those guards hear it, Julian thought. Right now, they're still watching the fires and the activity in the streets.

"Okay, bounce and fire on the numbers. Here we go. One!"

Julian leapt into the air, firing a rocket at one of the guard towers. He noted with satisfaction the two Skinnies in the tower hadn't even seen him until the rocket was on its way. They have about a second to live, he thought.

There are a total of twelve armed Skinnies in the compound (two each in four towers, and four on the ground). Each Skinny has an Ordnance value of 3.

The M.I. have achieved surprise. The Skinnies don't fire in the first round of the battle.

The M.I. fire using Chart C.

The Skinnies fire using Chart E, beginning in the second round of the fight.

The fight lasts three rounds. At the end of the third round, any surviving M.I. board the retrieval boat, and the boat takes off.

If there are no M.I. survivors, go to section 77.

If Julian is the only M.I. survivor, go to section 79.

If there are two or more M.I. survivors, go to section 78.

— 76 —

Julian first saw the boat as a tiny pinpoint of flame high in the sky. The sound followed in a few seconds. Better move before those guards hear it, Julian thought. Right now, they're still watching the fires and the activity in the streets.

Unknown to Julian, the guards had already spotted the squad moving into position and were just waiting for the men to leave cover.

"Okay, bounce and fire on the numbers. Here we go. One!"

Julian leapt into the air, firing a rocket at one of the guard towers. He noted with dismay that the two Skinnies in the tower immediately opened fire, right at him.

There are a total of twelve armed Skinnies in the compound (two each in four towers and four on the ground). Each Skinny has an Ordnance value of 3.

The Skinnies spot the M.I. moving into position. They open fire as soon as the M.I. move.

The M.I. fire using Chart C.

The Skinnies fire using Chart D.

The fight lasts for three rounds. At the end of the third

round, any surviving M.I. board the retrieval boat, and the boat takes off.

If there are no M.I. survivors, go to section 77.

If Julian is the only M.I. survivor, go to section 79.

If there are two or more M.I. survivors, go to section 78.

— 77 —

The firepower in the compound was too great for the squad to overcome. The Skinnies in the towers opened up with everything they had. Julian fought hard, but neither he nor his squad could throw their rockets and bombs fast enough.

Julian made it to the ground after his bounce over the fence and stayed alive long enough to see Woczinski buy his farm. After that, it was move and fire, move and fire, until you're hit, you're down, pain, oh the pain, and then the cold. . . .

With his last breath, knowing the squad was doomed, Julian saved the lives of the boat crew. Switching to his circuit for direct communication with the boat, he managed to choke out, "Abort retrieval."

Go to section 29.

— 78 —

"How the pilot got this boat lifted off again, I'll never know," Woczinski said.

"Yeah," grunted Julian.

He wanted to be alone, to think over his mistakes and to wonder if he should ever command anything more than a hand flamer again.

"Not too good. At least we made the boat," he finally said.

"From what I've heard, plenty of actions don't turn out too good," Woczinski replied. "I guess that's why they give us all this training and equipment—and citizenship if we stay alive long enough to claim it. If it was easy . . ." Woczinski's voice trailed off.

Yeah, thought Julian, if it was easy . . .

Go to section 110.

— 79 —

Julian landed from his bounce, fired his flamer at a Skinny standing not five feet away, and then heard the worst sound he'd ever heard in his life: a dull, metallic, ringing thud. Woczinski fell ten feet behind Julian. There was no need to go back and check his vital signs. One quick glance at the scattered remains was enough for Julian.

A wave of white-hot hatred and grief flooded through Julian's body. He hated Skinnies, hated them down deep, hated them with every fiber of his being.

He fired wildly at anything that looked like a Skinny.

His flamer fired again, and again, and again. All the while, during those five or so seconds that seemed like eternity, he realized the squad was doomed, the mission was doomed, and even the retrieval boat was doomed if it didn't take off soon.

Julian threw himself through the door of the boat, lobbing grenades out through the hatch as it sealed shut. Within seconds, he was aloft. The boat pilot had enough sense to leave him alone all the way back to the *Colonel Bowie,* alone with that special, senseless grief and guilt that afflict the sole survivor of a disaster.

Go to section 110.

— 80 —

Julian peered one last time at the guards. They were still watching the show being put on by the fires and the civilians in the streets to the north. Once in a while, one of them glanced toward the ground in the middle of the compound, then looked skyward.

Probably worrying about that retrieval beacon, Julian thought. Bet they're scared half silly thinking a boat's going to come down right on top of them.

"Okay. We all go at once. By the numbers. On 'one' we're over the fence, taking out guard towers, flaming any armed Skinnies on the ground. On 'two' we rush those doors and go straight inside. Flame anything that looks dangerous but remember, we want prisoners. And, we've got two minutes before the boat lands.

"Here we go. One!"

Julian soared into the air, fired a rocket at one guard tower, and slung the rocket launcher on his back. He readied his flamer and managed to get off a shot at one of the Skinny guards on the ground inside the fence. He hit the ground and rolled to avoid being knocked down by the explosion from his own squad's rockets, then was up and on his feet.

"Two!" Julian shouted, and dashed for the large doors in the west side of the building.

There are a total of twelve Skinnies outside the building (two each in the four guard towers and four on the ground). Each Skinny has an Ordnance value of 3.

The M.I. have achieved surprise, so the Skinnies do not fire in the first round of the fight.

The M.I. fire using Chart C.

The Skinnies fire using Chart E.

The combat lasts three rounds. At the end of the third round, any surviving M.I. dash inside the large R&D building.

If Julian is the sole surviving M.I., go to section 84.

If two or more M.I. survive, go to section 82.

If the M.I. are all killed, go to section 83.

— 81 —

Julian peered one last time at the guards. They still seemed to be watching the show put on by the fires and the civilians in the streets to the north. Once in a while, one of them glanced toward the ground in the middle of the compound, then looked skyward.

Probably worrying about that retrieval beacon, Julian thought. Bet they're scared half silly thinking a boat's going to come down right on top of them.

"Okay. We all go at once. By the numbers. On 'one' we're over the fence, taking out guard towers, flaming any armed Skinnies on the ground. On 'two' we rush those doors and go straight inside. Flame anything that looks dangerous but remember, we want prisoners. And, we've got two minutes before the boat lands.

"Here we go. One!"

Julian soared into the air, fired a rocket at one guard tower, and slung the rocket launcher onto his back. He readied his flamer and managed to get off a shot at one of the Skinny guards on the ground inside the fence. He hit the ground and rolled to avoid being knocked down by the explosion from his own squad's rockets, then was up and on his feet. That was when he noticed the Skinnies were definitely not surprised. Laser fire flashed everywhere at once!

"Two!" Julian shouted, and dashed for the large doors in the west side of the building.

There are a total of twelve Skinnies outside the building (two each in the four guard towers and four on the ground). Each Skinny has an Ordnance value of 3.

The M.I. fire using Chart C.

The Skinnies fire using Chart D.

The combat lasts three rounds. At the end of the third round, any surviving M.I. dash inside the large R&D building.

If Julian is the sole surviving M.I., go to section 84.

If two or more M.I. survive, go to section 82.

If the M.I. are all killed, go to section 83.

— 82 —

The large doors, even though shut tight, were no match for running men, each wearing a full ton of powered armor. The squad slammed through them with ease, pinning one Skinny civilian against the inside wall.

Shrieks and screams erupted at once from the glass-walled offices that lined the corridor extending in front of the M.I. troopers. Inside those offices, the squad could see Skinny civilians diving under desks, running for doors into other rooms, or grabbing communications devices. A few brave souls were still at their posts, working on what appeared to be computer terminals, no doubt destroying data files. One Skinny dared to dart into the corridor, carrying a large bundle of papers and files. It fled away from the troopers toward the interior of the building.

"Okay, let's grab some prisoners!" Julian shouted.

Even as he spoke, he spotted the four armed security guards emerging on the run, from a side corridor, their laser pistols at the ready. From somewhere in the building, a siren began wailing, its sound amplified by strategically placed speakers throughout the structure.

"Flamers only—too tight a space for grenades!" Julian's reminder was hardly necessary. Woczinski had his flamer at the ready and fired simultaneously with the guards.

There are four Skinny guards, each with an Ordnance value of 3.

The Skinnies fire using Chart E.

The M.I. fire using Chart B.

After two rounds, the Skinnies inside the building are

joined by half the survivors from the fight outside the building (from Section 80 or 81). After four rounds, the other half of the Skinny survivors from that fight join in. Continue this fight until either all the Skinnies or all the M.I. are dead.

If the M.I. win the fight, go to section 98.

If the Skinnies win the fight, go to section 99.

— 83 —

Julian never made it inside the door. Neither did the rest of the squad.

He never even knew if anyone heard him call "two!" because he immediately became very, very busy.

The guard towers weren't all knocked out. That left two Skinnies high above the open ground outside the building with plenty of opportunity to aim and fire their heavy lasers. Crowding against the sides of the building didn't give Julian's squad much cover. Grenades don't have to be accurately placed to be effective.

Julian's last words did save some lives, although not among the men he commanded. With his armor burned through and his skin flaming, he still managed to bite the mouth switch to open the circuit for direct communication with the retrieval boat.

His last words were "Abort retrieval."

Go to section 29.

— 84 —

The large doors, even though shut tight, were no match for a running man in a full ton of powered armor. Julian slammed through them with ease, pinning one Skinny civilian against the inside wall.

Shrieks and screams erupted from the glass-walled offices that lined the long corridor in front of Julian. Inside those offices, Julian saw Skinny civilians diving under desks, running for doors into other rooms, or grabbing communications devices. A few brave souls were still at their posts, working on what appeared to be computer terminals—no doubt destroying data files. One Skinny dared to dart into the corridor, carrying a large bundle of papers and files. It fled away from Julian toward the interior of the building.

"Squad, report!"

Julian called the command from reflex, but realized instantly that it was pointless. There was no squad anymore. He was alone in the entrance to a Skinny think-tank, and it was up to him to complete the mission.

Julian spotted four security guards coming around an interior corner the same moment they spotted him. His hand flamer crisped the fleeing civilian, files and all, just as the guards let fly with their laser pistols.

This can't last long, Julian thought, blasting what was left of the door behind him into slag to block any incoming Skinnies. Then he charged straight for the guards.

If Julian darts into an office to try to grab prisoners and take cover, go to section 95.

If Julian continues charging dead ahead at the guards, go to section 96.

— 85 —

Julian heard the explosion of his rocket hitting the jeep behind him. He was moving fast, on the bounce, and had already passed the Skinny patrol. No time to check for enemy casualties, he thought. But if we accomplish this mission, command won't mind a few gaps in the after-action report.

"Target complex dead ahead. I have it on visual at the top of my bounce," Woczinski called.

"Right. Let's start feeding some rockets into those guard towers," Julian replied, slapping another load into his launcher as he bounced over the top of a factory. The factory rooftop exploded behind him: bombs from his Y-rack kept his rear clear of any wandering, armed Skinnies.

"I see it now myself, Woczinski," Julian said, sending a rocket toward the southwest guard tower.

"Bounce right in! Take out the towers as you go and rush the west doors of the building. Let's move!"

The first laser fire from the guard towers sliced the air above Julian as he dropped at the end of his bounce. Then Julian heard the sound most loved by the M.I. but not so welcome, just yet, in this case: the retrieval beacon! The boat would land at Point D in just three minutes!

There are a total of twelve Skinnies outside the R&D building (two in each of the four guard towers and four on the ground). Each Skinny has an Ordnance value of 3. See Map 2 for details of the Skinny deployment.

The Skinnies fire using Chart E.

Julian's squad fires using Chart C.

The fight lasts only four rounds. At the end of the fourth

round, any surviving M.I. crash through the west doors of
the building and disappear inside.

If two or more M.I. survive, go to section 88.

If Julian is the sole M.I. survivor, go to section 84.

If all the M.I. are killed, go to section 89.

— 86 —

"I can't believe it!"

Julian allowed the despairing words to escape his lips. It
no longer mattered. No one was listening on the squad's
frequency, no one at all.

Despite a decent tactical plan, despite careful bouncing,
despite the degree of natural protection offered by the
powered armor, Julian had watched the remainder of his
squad be cut to pieces by the incredible marksmanship of
the Skinny patrol.

Julian knew his chances of survival were next to nothing
unless he surrendered to the Skinnies. Sure, I'm past their
patrol now, he thought, but there are more armed Skinnies
ahead, and a human in powered armor is going to be a
little conspicuous. If I call the retrieval boat and cancel
retrieval, I'll at least spare the boat crew the extreme risk
involved in their part of this operation.

Julian ducked through a rubbled hole in the wall of a
flaming factory and bit the comm-unit switch to get his
frequency for the retrieval boat.

"This is Corporal Penn. Mission aborted. Squad destroyed. Abort retrieval. Penn out."

"We hear you. Good luck, soldier," came a voice in
response.

It was the last voice Julian ever heard. Two Skinny strays from the patrol spotted him and gunned him down with laser fire even before the boat captain had switched off.

Go to section 29.

— 87 —

"I can't believe it!"

Julian let the words escape his lips. It didn't matter— there was no one else listening on the squad circuit.

Despite the squad's armor and careful bouncing, they were picked off in the air by the incredible marksmanship of the Skinny gunners in the jeeps and on the rooftops.

Julian Penn had underestimated his enemy, and that error ended his life.

Go to section 29.

— 88 —

The large doors, even though shut tight, were no match for the running men, each wearing a full ton of powered armor. The squad slammed through them with ease, pinning one Skinny civilian against the inside wall.

Shrieks and screams erupted at once from the glass-walled offices that lined the corridor extending in front of the M.I. troopers. Inside those offices, the squad could see Skinny civilians diving under desks, running for doors into other rooms, or grabbing communications devices. A few brave souls were still at their posts, working on what appeared to be computer terminals—no doubt destroying data files. One Skinny dared to dart into the corridor, carrying a large bundle of papers and files. It fled away from the troopers toward the interior of the building.

"Okay, let's grab some prisoners!" Julian shouted.

Even as he spoke, he spotted four armed security guards emerging on the run, from a side corridor, their laser pistols at the ready. From somewhere in the building, a siren began wailing, its sound amplified by strategically placed speakers throughout the structure.

"Flamers only—too tight a space for grenades!" Julian's reminder was hardly necessary. Woczinski had his flamer at the ready and fired simultaneously with the guards.

There are four Skinny guards, each with an Ordnance value of 3.

The Skinnies fire using Chart E.

The M.I. fire using Chart C.

After two rounds, the Skinnies inside the building are joined by half the survivors from the fight outside the building (from section 85). After four rounds, the other half of the Skinny survivors from that fight join in. Continue this fight until either all the Skinnies or all the M.I. are dead.

If the M.I. win the fight, go to section 98.

If the Skinnies win the fight, go to section 99.

— 89 —

Julian's squad bounced off the south and west sides of the Skinny compound's fence . . . and bounced to their deaths. Despite their superior individual firepower and equipment, they were simply outgunned by the well-prepared Skinnies.

Julian saw Woczinski die. The large, brave rookie, who had acted so like a veteran throughout this mission, took a direct hit from one of the tower lasers. He dropped from his bounce onto the hard pavement with a sickening, metallic "thunk." A nearby grenade explosion finished him.

Julian went down fighting. Despite the carnage all around him, he didn't forget his responsibilities. His dying words went out over the special circuit for contact with the retrieval boat. "Abort retrieval," he signaled, and saved the lives of the boat crew with his last words.

Go to section 29.

— 90 —

"Surprise is the whole idea. We'll sneak up ·on the target. At two hundred yards range, go to ground. Then we'll sneak in close, bounce once, hit those towers with rocket fire, and be inside the building before the Skinnies know what's hit them."

"I have the target complex on visual, coming up on two hundred yards range now."

"Okay, Woczinski. Everyone hits the ground at the end of this bounce. If you have civilian problems, use low bounces immediately and scatter fire pills to clear a path. Otherwise, try to stay out of sight of those towers."

Julian hit the ground, dashed to the side of a building, and flattened himself against it before looking around the corner. So far, so good. He ran between the cover of the buildings, sneaking a peek before moving on. In this way, he worked his way northeast. Julian checked his tactical display, which indicated the squad was closing on target as planned. No civilian problems; any workers in those buildings had already fled north or taken cover inside, Julian thought.

Roll two dice. If the result is the same as or less than the squad's Stealth value, go to section 102.

If the result is greater than the squad's Stealth value, go to section 100.

— **91** —

"Our chances of sneaking through the streets are almost nothing—too many civilians may be inside those buildings, and we don't how many of them are tied into some kind of civil-defense communications network. Move on the bounce, just like we were going to flame the target the same way we're flaming these other factory buildings. At about two hundred yards, concentrate rocket fire on those guard towers. Bounce right over that fence and rush the west doors of the building."

And hope this works, Julian added in his own mind.

Woczinski let loose the first rocket. The guard towers were not slow to respond.

There are eight Skinnies firing (two from each guard tower), each with an Ordnance value of 3.

The M.I. fire using Chart C.

The Skinnies fire using Chart E.

After four rounds, the squad is inside the fence. Four more Skinnies there join the fight. After this fifth round, any surviving M.I. enter the building and this encounter ends.

If two or more M.I. make it inside the building, go to section 107.

If Julian is the only M.I. to make it inside the building, go to section 106.

If all the M.I. are killed, go to section 29.

— 92 —

"Surprise is the whole idea. We'll sneak up on the target. At two hundred yards range, go to ground. Then we'll sneak in close, bounce once, hit those towers with rocket fire, and be inside the building before the Skinnies know what's hit them."

"I have the target complex on visual, coming up on two hundred yards range now."

"Okay, Woczinski. Everyone hits the ground at the end of this bounce. If you have civilian problems, use low bounces immediately and scatter fire pills to clear a path. Otherwise, try to stay out of sight of those towers."

Julian hit the ground, dashed to the side of a building, and flattened himself against it before looking around the corner. So far, so good. He ran between the cover of the buildings, sneaking a peek before moving on. In this way, he worked his way northeast. Julian checked his tactical display, which indicated the squad was closing on target as planned. No civilian problems; any workers in those buildings had already fled north or taken cover inside, Julian thought.

Roll two dice. If the result is the same as or less than the squad's Stealth value, go to section 103.

If the result is greater than the squad's Stealth value, go to section 101.

— 93 —

"Our chances of sneaking through the streets are almost nothing—too many civilians may be inside those buildings, and we don't know how many of them are tied into some kind of civil-defense communications network. Move on the bounce, just like we were going to flame the target the same way we're flaming these other factory buildings. At about two hundred yards, concentrate rocket fire on those guard towers. Bounce right over that fence and rush the west doors of the building."

And hope this works, Julian added in his own mind.

Woczinski let loose the first rocket. The guard towers were not slow to respond.

There are eight Skinnies firing (two from each guard tower), each with an Ordnance value of 3.

The M.I. fire using Chart C.

The Skinnies fire using Chart E.

After four rounds, the squad is inside the fence. Four more Skinnies there join the fight. After this fifth round, any surviving M.I. enter the building and this encounter ends.

If two or more M.I. make it inside the building, go to section 105.

If Julian is the only M.I. to make it inside the building, go to section 104.

If all the M.I. are killed, go to section 29.

— 94 —

The fight ended quickly. Julian sized up his losses, then pressed on.

"Let's move. The Bugs in the tunnel mouth will probably redeploy now that their Brain's plan has gone awry. If we hurry, we may catch them in the act."

Julian moved as rapidly as possible down the tunnel, praying for a glimpse of that major artery. Soon, he spotted it.

"Okay, this is it. Move up as quietly as possible, then into that artery, turn right, and advance flaming away. The artery looks wide enough for us to go four abreast. Men in front line down, alternating fire with those in back, then those in back advance, forming moving lines with continuous firing. Got it? Let's go!"

Roll two dice. If the result is equal to or less than the section's Stealth value, go to section 126.

If the result of the roll is higher than the section's Stealth value, go to section 118.

— 95 —

Julian dove through a glass door as laser fire ripped past him. Glass shards showered the Skinny at a computer terminal not five feet from Julian. The Skinny ducked its head instinctively—Skinny reflexes are similar to human—and Julian grabbed the Skinny's leg, pulled it to the floor with one clean jerk.

A quick roll, and Julian was atop the Skinny, ready to kill it by simply tightening the muscles of his left arm. He rolled onto his back just as the security guards reached the shattered glass door, laser pistols in hand.

Sure hope this Skinny is as important to them as it is to me right now, Julian thought. No way to communicate with them, but as long as this Skinny's between us, maybe they won't fire.

Julian sat up facing the guards. The Skinny in his arms screeched in fear as Julian's arm tightened a bit on its throat. With his free right hand, Julian raised his hand flamer as he brought himself and the Skinny to their feet.

A wave of the hand flamer backed the guards off. They gave ground slowly, never lowering their pistols.

Julian heard Skinnies shouting outside. A few seconds later, he heard the roar of the retrieval boat's engines as it came to land right in the middle of the Skinny parking area. At least, he thought, the lasers and grenades the Skinnies have outside don't have much of a chance of damaging the boat.

Julian eased out through the shattered glass door and put his back to the corridor wall, keeping his Skinny captive in front of his own body at all times. The security guards glanced at one another nervously. Julian eased toward the entrance, glancing back and forth from the guards to the outer door.

Have to keep this Skinny between me and their fire, he

told himself. Let's see . . . I've got to cross about twenty-five yards of open ground out there, and they'll be all over the place.

Oh well, if it was easy, they wouldn't need the M.I. to do it.

Julian was almost to the door to the outside when he heard the retrieval boat touch down. With a flick of a switch, he set his Y-rack on automatic, then whirled and faced down the corridor toward the security guards. Grenades spewed from his Y-rack through the open doorway into the parking area outside.

That should do it, Julian thought. He spun around and took a short bounce with the Skinny tucked under his left arm. His aim was to land right in front of the retrieval boat's ramp, which was just beginning to lower.

All the remaining Skinnies outside the R&D building (those not killed in the previous fighting outside) got one free round of fire against Julian. They fire using Chart E. Julian is too busy trying to get into the boat to return fire.

If Julian is killed, go to section 29.

If Julian is not killed, go to section 97.

— 96 —

Julian's charge was a charge into folly, something he realized an instant too late. Even as he closed with the Skinnies, hand flamer blazing away, he was cut down from behind by surviving Skinnies from outside. The broken door proved no obstacle to them.

Julian couldn't stifle his scream of pain as laser fire penetrated the back of his powered armor, burning through his spine and abdomen. Nor could he keep himself alive more than a few seconds. With a supreme effort of will-power, he bit the comm-unit switch and managed to open his direct channel to the retrieval boat.

Julian's last words were "Abort retrieval."

They were at once the most wonderful and the most horrible words that retrieval boat pilot had ever heard.

Go to section 29.

— 97 —

More laser fire, more explosions, a dash up the ramp, safety!

"Take off. I'm all that's left," Julian shouted.

His prisoner was quickly hustled to a cot and strapped down, as Julian collapsed. He felt the ship engines build-ing up power, felt the g-forces slamming him into the thick padding of the acceleration couch.

By the time the boat reached zero gee, Julian was trembling, and the trembling wouldn't stop. It was the trembling of guilt, grief, and rage at himself for leading Miller, Estrada, Woczinski, and LeClerc to their deaths.

Julian struggled to hold back his tears.

"That's all right, son," came the pilot's voice. "It's over now. You accomplished your mission."

Go to section 110.

— 98 —

The Skinnies poured in from everywhere, and the M.I. let them have it. Woczinski's first flamer blast crisped the Skinny civilian with the papers and successfully intimidated the Skinny guards. They dove for cover, firing as they went. Julian violated his own order and lobbed a grenade down the corridor after them, advanced about fifteen feet and crashed through a glass door.

Glass shards showered the Skinny working frantically at a computer in the large office. Julian dove to the floor as laser fire singed the air over his helmet, grabbed the Skinny by the leg, and pulled it down with one swift jerk. In seconds, Julian was standing again, the Skinny held in front of his own body in a death lock, while his free right hand sent fiery death out the shattered glass door in the direction of arriving Skinny reinforcements.

"They're coming in behind us," Woczinski shouted.

"No problem," Julian replied, bathing the outside doorway in flaming death.

Julian and the other M.I. crashed through doorway after doorway, avoiding the corridor and grabbing Skinny civilians as they passed. The civilians tended to behave themselves when a flamer was pointed their way. Woczinski burned down the first one who tried to run away, and the rest gave the M.I. no trouble.

The Skinnies never caught on. They kept dashing through the door from the outside and running down the corridor—perfect targets, even though they were moving. Julian kept his men in the offices, behind partial cover. The firefight became a turkey shoot.

The musical strains of the retrieval boat's beacon sounded thirty seconds before Julian noticed there weren't any more Skinnies shooting at them.

"Beacon!" he snapped. "Finish off resisters and make

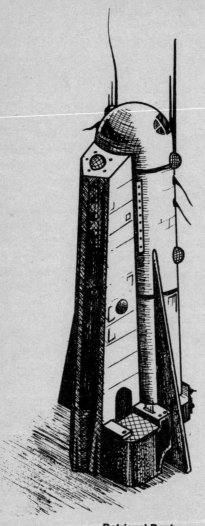

Retrieval Boat

your way back to the west door the way you came. Avoid the corridors. Herd your prisoners in front of you; use them for cover.''

They waited about a minute and a half for the retrieval boat. As soon as it touched down, Julian herded the prisoners toward it.

"Move in the middle of the prisoners; if there are any armed Skinnies around, they may hesitate to shoot into a crowd of their own."

If any armed Skinnies were around, they did hesitate. In fact, they didn't fire at all. In less than half a minute, the retrieval boat was loaded full with Skinny prisoners. Julian was the last man to board.

"Let's head home," he told the pilot with a grin.

"I'll drink to that, as soon as we get there," Woczinski chimed in.

Go to section 110.

— **99** —

The Skinnies poured in from everywhere, and the M.I. let them have it. Woczinski's first flamer blast crisped the Skinny civilian with the papers and successfully intimidated the Skinny guards. They dove for cover, firing as they went. Julian violated his own order and lobbed a grenade down the corridor after them, advanced about fifteen feet and crashed through a glass door.

Glass shards showered the Skinny working frantically at a computer in the large office. Julian dove to the floor as laser fire singed the air over his helmet, grabbed the Skinny by the leg, and pulled it down with one swift jerk. In seconds, Julian was standing again, the Skinny held in front of his own body in a death lock, while his free right hand sent fiery death out the shattered glass door in the direction of arriving Skinny reinforcements.

"They're coming in behind us," Woczinski shouted.

"No problem," Julian replied, bathing the outside doorway in flaming death.

Julian and the other M.I. crashed through doorway after doorway, avoiding the corridor and grabbing Skinny civilians as they passed. The civilians tended to behave themselves when a flamer was pointed their way. Woczinski burned down the first one who tried to run away, and the rest gave the M.I. no trouble.

But the Skinnies caught on quickly. Their troops stopped dashing through the smashed doors and down the corridor into the M.I.'s fire. They used covering fire to get through the doorways, then darted into offices and moved from desk to doorway to desk. It was a long, brutal chase. The M.I. herded their prisoners and tried to use them for cover while avoiding the corridors. Both sides paid, but the price the M.I. paid was final: they bought their farms.

Julian had the good sense to abort the retrieval boat before he died. No sense in risking the boat crew, he thought. It was the last thought he had.

Go to section 29.

— 100 —

The squad worked its way to positions about fifty yards from the compound fence. Julian sneaked a look around the corner of a warehouse. He couldn't see inside the fence, but he could see the top of the southwest guard tower. The guards seemed to be enjoying their view of the fires to the southwest and the fleeing civilians to the north.

"Okay. On 'one' we bounce and slam rockets at the

guard towers. Make it a good bounce; we should land inside the fence. Roll when you hit the pavement; you'll be close to our own rocket explosions. Come up with flamers ready and crisp anything that looks even vaguely hostile, then rush the west doors of the L-shaped building. Any questions?''

Woczinski was the only one to answer.

''Let's do it,'' he said.

''All right, *One!*'' Julian shouted over the comm unit.

The Skinny guards responded instantly. They had spotted the M.I. moving into position and were expecting a sudden sneak attack. Rockets leapt from M.I. launchers toward the towers, but laser fire answered almost simultaneously.

Julian hit the pavement inside the fence and rolled as explosions rocked the ground. He came up quickly, flamer ready.

''Inside those doors,'' he ordered. ''Now! Move!''

There are twelve Skinnies inside the compound but outside the building (two in each of the four guard towers and four on the ground, as shown on Map 2). Each Skinny has an Ordnance value of 3.

The M.I. fire using Chart C.

The Skinnies fire using Chart E.

The fight lasts for three rounds. After three rounds, any surviving M.I. run inside the L-shaped building.

If the M.I. are all killed, go to section 29.

If Julian is the sole M.I. survivor, go to section 106.

If two or more M.I. survive, go to section 107.

— 101 —

The squad worked its way to positions about fifty yards from the compound fence. Julian sneaked a look around the corner of a warehouse. He couldn't see inside the fence, but he could see the top of the southwest guard tower. The guards seemed to be enjoying their view of the fires to the southwest and the fleeing civilians to the north.

"Okay. On 'one' we bounce and slam rockets at the guard towers. Make it a good bounce; we should land inside the fence. Roll when you hit the pavement; you'll be close to our own rocket explosions. Come up with flamers ready and crisp anything that looks even vaguely hostile, then rush the west doors of the L-shaped building. Any questions?"

Woczinski was the only one to answer.

"Let's do it," he said.

"All right. *One!*" Julian shouted over the comm unit.

The Skinny guards responded instantly. They had spotted the M.I. moving into position and were expecting a sudden sneak attack. Rockets leapt from M.I. launchers toward the towers, but laser fire answered almost simultaneously.

Julian hit the pavement inside the fence and rolled as explosions rocked the ground. He came up quickly, flamer ready.

"Inside those doors," he ordered. "Now! Move!"

There are twelve Skinnies inside the compound but outside the building (two in each of the four guard towers, and four on the ground, as shown on Map 2). Each Skinny has an Ordnance value of 3.

The M.I. fire using Chart C.

The Skinnies fire using Chart D.

The fight lasts for three rounds. After three rounds, any surviving M.I. run inside the L-shaped building.

If the M.I. are all killed, go to section 29.

If Julian is the sole M.I. survivor, go to section 104.

If two or more M.I. survive, go to section 105.

— 102 —

The squad worked its way to positions about fifty yards from the compound fence. Julian sneaked a look around the corner of a warehouse. He couldn't see inside the fence, but he could see the top of the southwest guard tower. The guards seemed to be enjoying their view of the fires to the southwest and the fleeing civilians to the north.

"Okay. On 'one' we bounce and slam rockets at the guard towers. Make it a good bounce; we should land inside the fence. Roll when you hit the pavement; you'll be close to our own rocket explosions. Come up with flamers ready and crisp anything that looks even vaguely hostile, then rush the west doors of the L-shaped building. Any questions?"

Woczinski was the only one to answer.

"Let's do it," he said.

"All right. *One!*" Julian shouted over the comm unit.

The Skinny guards didn't have time to respond. They weren't expecting a sudden sneak attack. Rockets leapt from M.I. launchers toward the towers.

Julian hit the pavement inside the fence and rolled as explosions rocked the ground. He came up quickly, flamer ready.

"Inside those doors," he ordered. "Now! Move!"

There are twelve Skinnies inside the compound but outside the building (two in each of the four guard towers and four on the ground, as shown on Map 2). Each Skinny has an Ordnance value of 3.

The M.I. have achieved surprise. The Skinnies do not fire during the first round of the fight.

The M.I. fire using Chart C.

The Skinnies fire using Chart F.

The fight lasts for three rounds. After three rounds, any surviving M.I. run inside the L-shaped building.

If the M.I. are all killed, go to section 29.

If Julian is the sole M.I. survivor, go to section 106.

If two or more M.I. survive, go to section 107.

— 103 —

The squad worked its way to positions about fifty yards from the compound fence. Julian sneaked a look around the corner of a warehouse. He couldn't see inside the fence, but he could see the top of the southwest guard tower. The guards seemed to be enjoying their view of the fires to the southwest and the fleeing civilians to the north.

"Okay. On 'one' we bounce and slam rockets at the guard towers. Make it a good bounce; we should land inside the fence. Roll when you hit the pavement; you'll be close to our own rocket explosions. Come up with flamers ready and crisp anything that looks even vaguely hostile, then rush the west doors of the L-shaped building. Any questions?''

Woczinski was the only one to answer.

"Let's do it," he said.

"All right. *One!*" Julian shouted over the comm unit.

The Skinny guards didn't have time to respond. They weren't expecting a sudden sneak attack. Rockets leapt from M.I. launchers toward the towers.

Julian hit the pavement inside the fence and rolled as explosions rocked the ground. He came up quickly, flamer ready.

"Inside those doors," he ordered. "Now! Move!"

There are twelve Skinnies inside the compound but outside the building (two in each of the four guard towers and four on the ground, as shown on Map 2). Each Skinny has an Ordnance value of 3.

The M.I. have achieved surprise. The Skinnies do not fire during the first round of the fight.

The M.I. fire using Chart C.

The Skinnies fire using Chart F.

The fight lasts for three rounds. After three rounds, any surviving M.I. run inside the L-shaped building.

If the M.I. are all killed, go to section 29.

If Julian is the sole M.I. survivor, go to section 104.

If two or more M.I. survive, go to section 105.

— 104 —

The large doors at the west end of the building were shut tightly, but proved no match for Julian. Most doors can't stand up to a running man who happens to be wearing about a ton of powered armor.

Julian crashed through the doors and quickly saw his opportunity. Ahead of him stretched a long, wide hallway lined with glass-walled offices.

Screams and shrieks of surprise and panic echoed from those offices seconds after Julian entered. Through the glass walls, he could see dozens of Skinnies, most of them diving for cover. A few bold ones were quickly manning communications equipment or heading for computer terminals—no doubt to dump valuable secret data—or gathering up papers and files. One valiant Skinny soul even dared to enter the corridor, clutching a bundle of documents and running for its life toward the interior of the building.

In the two seconds it took Julian to size up the situation, the situation changed. Four armed Skinnies—probably security guards, Julian thought—emerged from a side corridor on the run, laser pistols at the ready.

Okay, thought Julian. Let's see what a squad of one can do.

Laser fire ripped down the hall, answered by streams of flame.

There are four Skinnies with an Ordnance value of 3 each. After four rounds of fighting, these Skinnies are joined by half the Skinnies who survived the fight outside the building (see Section 93, 101, or 103). After the eighth round, the remaining Skinnies from outside join the fight.

The skinnies fire using Chart E.

Julian fires using Chart B.

If Julian is killed, go to section 29.

If Julian survives, go to section 111.

— 105 —

The large doors at the west end of the building were shut tightly, but proved no match for the rushing M.I. Most doors can't stand up to a group of running men, each wearing about a ton of powered armor.

Julian crashed through the doors first and quickly saw his opportunity. Ahead of him stretched a long, wide hallway lined with glass-walled offices.

Screams and shrieks of surprise and panic echoed from those offices seconds after the M.I. entered. Through the glass walls, Julian could see dozens of Skinnies, most of them diving for cover. A few bold ones were quickly manning communications equipment or heading for computer terminals—no doubt to dump valuable secret data—or gathering up papers and files. One valiant Skinny soul even dared to enter the corridor, clutching a bundle of documents and running for its life toward the interior of the building.

In the two seconds it took Julian to size up the situation, the situation changed. Four armed Skinnies—probably security guards, Julian thought—emerged from a side corridor on the run, laser pistols at the ready.

"Flame 'em!" Julian called. "Then take cover and take prisoners!"

Laser fire ripped down the hall, answered by streams of flame.

There are four Skinnies with an Ordnance value of 3 each. After four rounds of fighting, these Skinnies are joined by half the Skinnies who survived the fight outside the building (see section 93, 101, or 103). After the eighth round, the remaining Skinnies from outside join the fight.

The Skinnies fire using Chart F.

The M.I. fire using Chart B.

If all the M.I. are killed, go to section 29.

If Julian is the sole M.I. survivor, go to section 111.

If two or more M.I. survive, go to section 113.

— 106 —

The large doors at the west end of the building were shut tightly, but proved no match for Julian. Most doors can't stand up to a running man who happens to be wearing about a ton of powered armor.

Julian crashed through the doors and quickly saw his opportunity. Ahead of him stretched a long, wide hallway lined with glass-walled offices.

Screams and shrieks of surprise and panic echoed from those offices seconds after Julian entered. Through the glass walls, he could see dozens of Skinnies, most of them diving for cover. A few bold ones were quickly manning communications equipment or heading for computer terminals—no doubt to dump valuable secret data—or gathering up papers and files. One valiant Skinny soul even dared to enter the corridor, clutching a bundle of documents and running for its life toward the interior of the building.

In the two seconds it took Julian to size up the situation, the situation changed. Four armed Skinnies—probably security guards, Julian thought—emerged from a side corridor on the run, laser pistols at the ready.

Okay, thought Julian. Let's see what a squad of one can do.

Laser fire ripped down the hall, answered by streams of flame.

There are four Skinnies with an Ordnance value of 3 each. After four rounds of fighting, these Skinnies are joined by half the Skinnies who survived the fight outside the building, as described in section 91, 100, or 102. After the eighth round, the remaining Skinnies from outside join the fight.

The Skinnies fire using Chart E.

Julian fires using Chart B.

If Julian is killed, go to section 29.

If Julian survives, go to section 108.

— 107 —

The large doors at the west end of the building were shut tightly, but proved no match for the rushing M.I. Most doors can't stand up to a group of running men, each wearing about a ton of powered armor.

Julian crashed through the doors first and quickly saw his opportunity. Ahead of him stretched a long, wide hallway lined with glass-walled offices.

Screams and shrieks of surprise and panic echoed from those offices seconds after the M.I. entered. Through the glass walls, Julian saw dozens of Skinnies, most of them diving for cover. A few bold ones were quickly manning communications equipment or heading for computer terminals—no doubt to dump valuable secret data—or gathering up papers and files. One valiant Skinny soul even dared to enter the corridor, clutching a bundle of documents and running for its life toward the interior of the building.

In the two seconds it took Julian to size up the situation, the situation changed. Four armed Skinnies—probably security guards, Julian thought—emerged from a side corridor on the run, laser pistols at the ready.

"Flame 'em!" Julian called. "Then take cover and take prisoners!"

Laser fire ripped down the hall, answered by streams of flame.

There are four Skinnies with an Ordnance value of 3 each. After four rounds of fighting, these Skinnies are joined by half the Skinnies who survived the fight outside the building, as described in section 91, 100, or 102. After the eighth round, the remaining Skinnies from outside join the fight.

The Skinnies fire using Chart E.

The M.I. fire using Chart B.

If all the M.I. are killed, go to section 29.

If Julian is the sole M.I. survivor, go to section 108.

If two or more M.I. survive, go to section 109.

— 108 —

"I'll never understand it as long as I live," Julian said out loud. No danger of demoralizing the others now with that kind of talk, he thought bitterly.

By all rational standards, his survival was a miracle. After single-handedly holding off what seemed like the entire Skinny army in the think-tank offices, Julian was not only alive, but had taken four prisoners.

The fighting was a nightmare. First there were the Skinny guards inside the building. Julian flamed them, then threw himself through a glass wall into a Skinny office. He grabbed his first prisoner there—a Skinny who was working frantically at a computer terminal. The Skinny was a civilian, no match in hand-to-hand combat for a trained M.I. in powered armor.

The armed Skinnies backed off after that. Maybe they were afraid of hitting Julian's prisoner, because Julian unashamedly used it as a shield for his own body. The fighting went from office to office, Julian running, dodging, flaming, and lobbing grenades at any Skinnies silly enough to run down the corridors in groups. Somehow, when it was all over, he had four prisoners.

Now, he waited for the retrieval beacon, and when the familiar sound came, he edged carefully toward the west door, his back against the wall, one Skinny prisoner held tightly against his body, the others covered with the hand flamer in his free right hand.

The boat came down right on schedule. Julian motioned one prisoner out the door toward the boat. No one took a shot or rushed the door, so he herded the rest out and finally came out himself, still holding the final prisoner as a shield.

Laser fire erupted from all sides.

The Skinny patrol, Julian thought. It found us after all.

There are sixteen Skinnies waiting in ambush for any M.I. who leaves the building. Each Skinny has an Ordnance value of 3.

The Skinnies fire using Chart F.

Julian fires using Chart B.

The first casualty inflicted by Skinny fire is the prisoner Julian is holding. The second casualty is Julian himself.

The fight lasts three rounds. At the end of three rounds, Julian and his prisoners board the retrieval boat.

If Julian is killed, go to section 29.

If Julian makes it aboard the boat, go to section 112.

— 109 —

Julian dodged laser bursts, dove through a glass wall into a Skinny office, and slid across the floor. Shards of glass from the wall showered a Skinny working frantically at a computer terminal. The Skinny ducked its head—Skinny reflexes are in some ways very similar to humans'.

Julian grabbed the Skinny by the ankle. One swift motion pulled the screaming humanoid to the floor. Three seconds later, both were on their feet. Julian had his left arm wrapped around the Skinny's throat; a mere tightening of the pressure would kill the creature. His right hand was free, and already death leapt from his flamer into a group of Skinny security guards taking cover across the hall.

The other M.I. took their lead from Julian, smashing through the glass walls, grabbing prisoners and using them for cover, crashing through more doors, grabbing anything that looked valuable for military intelligence, taking more prisoners.

Meanwhile, armed Skinnies were in the hallways, firing at the dodging, covered M.I. and taking worse then they gave. Skinny reinforcements rushed in through the shattered west doors of the building. Woczinski lobbed grenades to cut them down in the doorway.

Slowly, the battle died out and Julian, herding several prisoners when the firing stopped, realized the M.I. had won.

"Any hostile fire?" he asked.

"Haven't seen or heard an armed Skinny for about thirty seconds," Woczinski replied.

"Okay. We'll make for those west doors, but stay inside the offices and use the prisoners for cover. When the retrieval boat lands, we'll herd them inside and be on our merry way."

The civilian prisoners seemed docile enough, Julian thought. In the minutes that passed before the retrieval beacon announced the imminent arrival of the boat, Julian studied his catch. These Skinnies looked older, in human terms, than the Skinny fighting troops. They weren't in the best shape physically; even a human eye could judge that. And they were quiet . . . very quiet.

At last the beacon sounded. Three minutes later and right on schedule, the retrieval boat descended to land on the parking lot.

"All right, let's move 'em out. Stay behind the prisoners just in case, though," Julian ordered.

The M.I. had only twenty-five yards of open ground to cross to reach the retrieval boat. The first prisoners were herded out the doorway before the boat ramp was even down. Julian stepped out in their midst, and laser fire erupted from all sides.

"Ambush!" Julian yelled, readying his flamer.

"Damn! It's the Skinny patrol. They must have figured out we'd be here," Woczinski volunteered.

The Skinny patrol consists of sixteen Skinnies, each with an Ordnance value of 3.

The Skinnies fire using Chart D.

The M.I. fire using Chart B.

Each M.I. herds four Skinny prisoners. The Skinny regulars are firing regardless of the risk of hitting their own people. The first M.I. casualty, and every second casualty thereafter, is actually a Skinny prisoner.

The combat lasts four rounds. At the end of the fourth round, any surviving M.I. and their prisoners board the retrieval boat.

If all the M.I. are killed, go to section 29.

If any M.I. survive, go to section 112.

— 110 —

"Sergeant Julian Penn, reporting for duty as ordered, sir."

This lieutenant looks busy, at least I'll say that for him, Julian thought.

"Hmmm. At ease, Sergeant. Take a seat outside. I'll be with you in a minute."

Julian eased into a seat outside the lieutenant's tiny office, lay his head back against the wall, and listened. The office walls on Sanctuary were notoriously paper thin, and every NCO used this method of finding out what was about to happen. The lieutenant's little cubicle was one of several with access to a larger central room where orderlies and clerks handled the necessary paperwork of the Second Battalion, Second Regiment, First Division. And not one of those orderlies or clerks did paperwork for a living. Every one of them was a combat veteran and would be dropping again on the battalion's next mission. In the M.I., *everybody* fights, from the cook to the chaplain.

Julian's wandering gaze caught that of the corporal at a nearby desk. The tall, thin man grinned at him. "What's the matter, Sarge? Can't wait to hear the news from the horse's mouth?"

"Well," Julian replied, returning the smile, "a man can't wait to hear the gossip from lower ratings now, can he?"

Scuttlebutt remained the one aspect of a soldier's life that the M.I. could not eliminate. In every barracks on every base, every private seemed to have an undying thirst for information, and the rumor mill kept that thirst satisfied. Sometimes the stories were true and sometimes they weren't. M.I. were more careful than most to keep false rumors at a minimum, so the grapevine was considered all the more valuable because of its accuracy.

The past two months had given Julian an ample demonstration of the grapevine's power. That demonstration had started almost as soon as he reached Fleet Base at Sanctuary after the raid on the Skinny think-tank. Nothing that was said aboard the *Colonel Bowie* on the trip back had prepared him for what met him at the base.

The trip back had been tough for Julian. He was naturally glad he had survived and took pride in some of the decisions he had made. But the carnage of the raid affected him, too. Boot camp had taught him that war wasn't some glamorous dream. The raid on Birgu had taught him that men in command must make tough decisions. But the raid on the Skinnies had shown him plenty of death at first hand. Even if a lot of the dead were aliens, the enemy, it was different than killing Bugs. Bugs seemed like . . . well . . . bugs. Skinnies were oddly human.

After reporting for debriefing on the *Colonel Bowie*, Julian had spent most of the time to himself, thinking about the meaning of killing, of ordering men to kill, of sending men to meet their deaths. He decided that he didn't much like it. Then he remembered why he, and a lot of men who were better than he, were doing it.

One of his instructors in boot camp had quoted a veteran M.I. That sentence summed up his thoughts perfectly:

"The best things in life are beyond money: their price is agony and sweat and devotion . . . and the price demanded for the most precious of all things in life is life itself—ultimate cost for perfect value."

Julian still wasn't sure what the best things in life were, but he found that he quietly believed somewhere deep inside, that there were things in life worth that ultimate price. Sure, soldiers will always complain about the soft life of civilians at home, safe in their beds, while the soldiers man the front lines of defense. But that was the whole point—keeping a way of life based upon decency, duty, and responsibility. Without that way of life, all the higher values that had motivated so many peaceful dreamers would vanish beneath the conqueror's sword. That was the lesson of history, and it didn't matter whether the conqueror happened to be a megalomaniac human, a coerced Skinny, or a brainy Bug.

It was in this philosophical frame of mind that Julian was granted three days' leave on Sanctuary, where he learned about the power of the grapevine.

It started as soon as his leave orders were confirmed. He was strolling out of the Second Battalion lieutenant's office—the same office he was in today, but on that day the lieutenant was a different lieutenant—when a clerk looked up from his desk and called, "You Penn?"

"Yes, Corporal Julian Penn. You have something for me?"

"A message. There was some ship's surgeon's assistant in here the other day, off the *El Alamein,* I think. Said she was looking for a Corporal Penn."

Brenda!

Julian's philosophical outlook brightened considerably. I may not know much about logic or metaphysics, but there's one thing I know I'd gladly fight for, he thought.

"Thank you, Corporal. Do you recall the precise message?" Julian tried to keep his voice calm and his face expressionless. If he didn't, he'd be taking a ribbing all the way out to the street.

"You're a cool customer, Penn," the corporal said with a smile. "I told her you were expected to report here today, and that she could probably catch you at this office. She a friend of yours?"

"Yes, she's a friend of mine, and if you want to be one, you'll let the subject drop right there."

"Okay, okay. I don't blame you. Wouldn't mind being among the wounded in *her* sick bay myself. Well, slick down your hair, Corporal Julian Penn. She's waiting outside."

Julian may have set a new speed record in covering that particular stretch of terrain between the corporal's desk and the street outside the M.I. Headquarters building. He took the steps down to the street in only three bounds, as if he were still in powered armor, and then came to a clumsy stop as he almost crashed into the object of his attentions.

"Well, soldier, I hope you're not so awkward in combat."

"Brenda! I'm, I'm, uh, I'm so glad to see you! Uh . . . how are you?"

"Oh Julian, you've changed in every way, and you haven't changed." Brenda's friendly laughter was the sweetest music Julian had ever heard—with the possible exception of a retrieval beacon. "Come on, soldier, let's get some lunch."

Lunch was delightful for Julian. Brenda's conversation was, as always, interesting, witty, and intelligent. She described her duties—not always the most pleasant, caring for the wounded and dying—and Julian could tell from her words, her tone, her face, everything about her, that she at least hadn't changed.

It was midway through lunch that Julian noticed what was bothering him. He had regressed! A few moments before seeing her he had been a combat veteran, proud, confident, perhaps a bit down and tending to muse about things, but a person who knew who he was and what he was doing. Now, all of a sudden, he was a love-sick teen again. He didn't like the feeling, but at the same time he relished it.

The feeling suddenly vanished when the tough subject came up.

"That's enough about me," Brenda said with finality. "Now Julian, there's something I really want you to know. About Paolo."

Oh no, thought Julian. Here it comes.

"Julian, I know you handled the situation in the best way you possibly could. You made a hard decision. I'm certain that you didn't let any silly personal feelings interfere. So if you were worried about how I'd feel, put your mind at ease."

"You mean, you don't think less of me because of what happened?"

"No Julian. In fact, I think more of you now, and more frequently, than ever."

"Oh." Julian sat silent, stunned with relief. Something vague was troubling the back of his mind. Eventually, it worked its way to his consciousness. "Say! How did you hear about the thing with Paolo?"

"News travels fast in the M.I., and in the Navy. Surprised you don't know that yet, Sergeant Penn."

"No, no, I'm just a corporal, Brenda."

"Not after this leave. Where have you been, Julian?

Don't you hear anything on those troop carriers?'' Her smile told him she was pleased, teasing him gently, and that she, at least, believed his promotion was a sure thing.

"Listen, Brenda, you can't always believe—"

"Sure, you can't always believe the scuttlebutt. I just happen to know this is true, because I checked it out with an officer. You'll get your sergeant's stripes when they present your Citation for Valor in front of the whole battalion, soon as you're back from leave.''

"Citation for Valor?''

"Come on, Julian, relax! You earned it. How many men could lead a mission like your last one and come back alive? When the story of that operation reached Fleet Base, you became something of a hero.''

"Guess I'm the last one to know,'' Julian replied glumly.

"What's the matter?''

"Listen Brenda, I don't feel like any hero,'' Julian said, perhaps more sharply than he would have liked. "I just did my duty as best I could, probably not as well as some better men could have done it, but as best I could under the circumstances. If I've learned anything, I've learned that no one becomes a hero by thinking about it. When you're in combat, you just do what you have to do. When you're in command in action, you don't think about what it means, and you don't think about the dying. You just think about what has to be done, now, to get the job done.''

"Julian.''

"Yes, Brenda?''

"Do you remember when you wanted to a run a store?''

"Huh?'' Julian's startled reply was involuntary. Her remarks had stunned him even more than news of the promotion and the citation. Julian remembered that somewhere, back in the days before Caesar was stabbed in the Senate, some child who was a distant relative of his had wanted to run a store. "Uh, yeah, I think so.''

"Do you remember the plans you had then?''

It came back in a flood—that day that seemed so long ago, before the pain, the fighting, the deaths—the day he had tried to propose and ended up joining the Mobile Infantry as a result.

"Yes, I remember."

"What do you say we get to work on those plans after you graduate from Officer Candidate School? Not the part about running a store. Just the part about us. I've been waiting, Julian. What do you think?"

"I think you're right," Julian said softly.

"Corporal Julian Penn!"

A big, loud voice boomed Julian's name at the most inappropriate moment—he had just leaned across the table to plant a soft kiss on his fiancée. Julian looked up to see a large, burly, florid-faced man standing by the table, his fists planted squarely on his hips.

"Brennan!"

"Hello, Corporal Penn. Or should I say, Sergeant Penn?" The big man extended his open right hand. "I hear we're going to be serving together again. Wanted to tell you I was glad to hear that."

Of course, it had all been true. Julian did get his sergeant's stripes and a Citation for Valor. Now he was back at Headquarters, waiting for reassignment.

Yes, the grapevine, Julian mused, as he waited for the lieutenant to call him in. Word does travel fast. But so far this time, Julian had no idea what was in store for him. The lieutenant wasn't talking in his office, and Julian had been unable to hear anything.

"Sergeant Penn, you can come in now," the lieutenant called.

"Sergeant Julian Penn, reporting for duty as ordered, sir," Julian snapped crisply.

"Sit down, Penn. I'm Lieutenant Abram Weiss. I believe we've served together once before."

"Yes, sir."

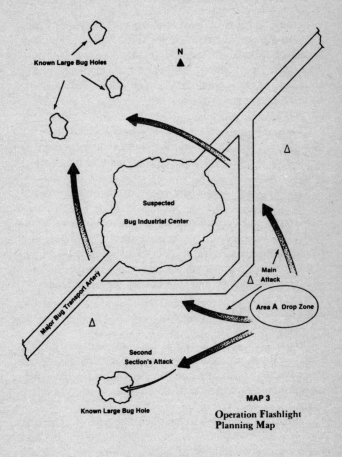

Known Large Bug Holes

N

Suspected

Bug Industrial Center

Main
Attack

Area A Drop Zone

Major Bug Transport Artery

Second
Section's Attack

Known Large Bug Hole

MAP 3

Operation Flashlight
Planning Map

△ Listening Devices

Scale: ¼" = 500 yards

"Yes. Back when I was as green as grass, just out of OCS, and you were a new squad leader. A lot's happened since then."

"Yes, sir."

"I'm afraid there's been another reorganization, Penn. I'm commanding a platoon now, Third Platoon, Company D, Second Battalion, Second Regiment, First Division. You're in that platoon, and as of this moment, you're commanding my second section. You'll have three squads, fifteen men counting yourself."

"Very good, sir."

"I hoped you'd be pleased. Now here's what you won't hear through the scuttlebutt. We're moving out tomorrow for Birgu. We've been there before; this will be a sort of homecoming."

"Birgu! That was where we picked up that special talent."

"Right. And he provided us with some good information. We have reason to believe there's a major Bug manufacturing and storage facility underground on Birgu. We believe the Skinnies ship laser weapons to the Bugs for storage there, and we intend to destroy the entire facility."

Look at Map 3 as you read on.

"Here's a map of the area we'll hit and our general plan. We'll be part of an even larger operation—taking out this particular facility is just our platoon's job—but information on this mission is strictly on a need-to-know basis.

"Now, our platoon will land here, in Area A. The first section will sweep slowly in a northwesterly direction toward that concentration of known Bug holes. Those are major holes spotted by the special talent, ones the Bugs normally use to deploy troops onto the surface. We're hoping the Bugs will come up to meet us. We'll have the Second Platoon on our right and the First on our left.

They'll be sweeping in the same general direction, off map. Should be enough to engage the Bugs when they come up from those holes, hopefully flanking them. We want them to send up as many as possible.

"The reason for drawing them out is your section's assignment. You'll move southwest, as shown here on the map, toward another major Bug hole. You will enter that hole and work your way toward the major Bug transport artery. The special talent sensed it while he was on Birgu. He thinks it may be pretty deep, but we don't know how deep.

"At this point, we're hoping the only Bug troops down there will be their reserves for this sector. You hit the transport artery, move into the industrial facility, and destroy it. Then get out however you can."

"How much time will we have?" Julian asked.

"We can stick around up to two hours, no longer."

"Special equipment?"

"You'll have a new nerve gas—it's called 'Tanglefoot'—in grenade form. We don't know how effective it will be against the Bugs. Your section will also be assigned three listening devices. You can plant these on the surface; they may help pick up bug traffic in their tunnels underground. Suggested locations for planting them are shown on the map, the final decision is up to you."

"Right. Any more information on the tunnel network in this area?"

"Sorry, no. You'll have to go by dead reckoning and luck."

"We'll do our best."

"Work out your tactical plan and go over it with me on board the ship tomorrow."

"Yes sir."

Julian left the lieutenant's office with a sinking feeling. Fifteen lives going down a Bug hole into uncharted tunnels. Oh great! Well, better get to work on a plan.

Julian spent the rest of the day poring over everything

he could lay his hands on about fighting in Bug tunnels. There wasn't much to go on, and what there was didn't sound good.

Bug tunnels are labyrinths. More than one squad had simply disappeared down them, gotten lost, been swallowed up in the ground. Humans tend to become easily disoriented in underground settings, and Bug tunnels are alien, hostile underground settings.

Some scientists believed the Bugs were able to make new tunnels very, very quickly. Julian confirmed that idea from his own experience. He remembered seeing Bugs come boiling up to the surface on Birgu, creating new holes and crawling out of them in seconds. No way to estimate their true speed through rock, though.

Another special problem was communication. Men who are more than a few yards underground can't use their comm units to talk to men on the surface. In the tunnels, the comm units have a much shorter range than normal, and the feedback is terrific, a real danger to eardrums if people started shouting.

The listening devices could pick up Bug movement. Bug tunneling makes a "frying bacon" noise that even a novice operator could recognize in an instant.

Finally, the Bugs prefer to fight in their tunnels. They'll send forces to the surface to combat raiders but usually keep a reserve underground, just in case.

Using this information, Julian formulated two plans of attack.

Plan A: The section will sacrifice firepower for security. One squad of five men will plant listening posts in the suggested areas. Three of the men can man the posts while the other two rove to provide fire support in case Bugs tunnel up unexpectedly. A second squad will be strung out along the line of march underground, with one man very near the surface. If the Bug tunnels were relatively straight— and there was a good chance they would be this near to a major underground artery—the strung-out squad could provide a communications link by comm unit with the men on the surface. The remaining squad will be the real attack force, the group designated to hit the target.

Plan B: The section will sacrifice security for firepower and numbers. Rather than divide up the men, the section will move and fight as a single unit. No men will be left topside. Napoleon used to recommend mass and momentum: the entire group will enter the hole quickly—no time wasted to deploy listening devices—and ramrod its way straight to the target.

Under both plans, one man in each squad is detailed to memorize the turns taken in the tunnel as the squad advances.

Record the following information about Julian's new command:

Manpower: 15
Ordnance: 7
Melee: 5
Stealth: 8
Morale: Special

To determine the section's Morale, take the last recorded morale for Julian's squad in the raid on the Skinny R&D facility. Add one for Julian's Citation for Valor. Add an additional point for each member of that squad who survived the mission. Finally, add one point if any Skinny prisoners were brought back. In no circumstances can the sections Morale be higher than 10.

Key personnel in Julian's section are:

Corporal Brennan, assistant section leader
Corporal Johnson, squad leader
Corporal Antonini, squad leader
Corporal Maalo, squad leader

If Julian chooses to use Plan A, go to section 114.

If Julian chooses to use Plan B, go to section 115.

— 111 —

"I'll never understand it as long as I live," Julian said out loud. No danger of demoralizing the others now with that kind of talk, he thought bitterly.

By all rational standards, his survival was a miracle. After single-handedly holding off what seemed like the entire Skinny army in the think-tank offices, Julian was not only alive, but had taken four prisoners.

The fighting was a nightmare. First there were the Skinny guards inside the building. Julian flamed them, then threw himself through a glass wall into a Skinny office. He grabbed his first prisoner there—a Skinny who was working frantically at a computer terminal. The Skinny was a civilian, no match in hand-to-hand combat for a trained M.I. in powered armor.

The armed Skinnies backed off after that. Maybe they were afraid of hitting Julian's prisoner, because Julian unashamedly used it as a shield for his own body. The fighting went from office to office, Julian running, dodging, flaming, and lobbing grenades at any Skinnies silly enough to run down the corridors in groups. Somehow, when it was all over, he had four prisoners.

Now, he waited for the retrieval beacon, and when the familiar sound came, he edged carefully toward the west door, his back against the wall, one Skinny prisoner held tightly against his body, the others covered with the hand flamer in his free right hand.

The boat came down right on schedule. Julian motioned one prisoner out the door toward the boat. No one took a shot or rushed the door, so he herded the rest out and finally came out himself, still holding the final prisoner as a shield. The miracle continued. Nothing happened.

"Made it!" Julian thought, as the retrieval boat ramp swung up. Inside the boat, the Skinny prisoners were quickly strapped down to acceleration couches.

"Take off, pilot," Julian sang out.

I did it. I led a suicide mission and pulled it off, Julian mused as the g-force pushed his body into the thick padding of his couch. Got to remember about citations for some of the fellows.

Go to section 110.

— 112 —

"Made it!" Julian thought as the retrieval boat ramp swung up. Inside the boat, the Skinny prisoners were quickly strapped down onto acceleration couches.

"Take off, pilot," Julian sang out.

I did it. I led a suicide mission and pulled it off, Julian mused as the g-force pushed his body into the thick padding of his couch. Got to remember about citations for some of the fellows.

Go to section 110.

— 113 —

Julian dodged laser bursts, dove through a glass wall into a Skinny office, and slid across the floor. Shards of

glass from the wall showered a Skinny working frantically at a computer terminal. The Skinny ducked its head—
Skinny reflexes are in some ways very similar to humans'.

Julian grabbed the Skinny by the ankle. One swift motion pulled the screaming humanoid to the floor. Three
seconds later, both were on their feet. Julian had his left
arm wrapped around the Skinny's throat; a mere tightening
of the pressure would kill the creature. His right hand was
free, and already death leapt from his flamer into a group
of Skinny security guards taking cover across the hall.

The other M.I. took their lead from Julian, smashing
through the glass walls, grabbing prisoners and using them
for cover, crashing through more doors, grabbing anything
that looked valuable for military intelligence, taking more
prisoners.

Meanwhile, armed Skinnies were in the hallways, firing
at the dodging, covered M.I. and taking worse than they
gave. Skinny reinforcements rushed in through the shattered west doors of the building. Woczinski lobbed grenades to cut them down in the doorway.

Slowly, the battle died out and Julian, herding several
prisoners when the firing stopped, realized the M.I. had
won.

"Any hostile fire?" he asked.

"Haven't seen or heard an armed Skinny for about
thirty seconds," Woczinski replied.

"Okay. We'll make for those west doors, but stay
inside the offices and use the prisoners for cover. When
the retrieval boat lands, we'll herd them inside and be on
our merry way."

The civilian prisoners seemed docile enough, Julian
thought. In the minutes that passed before the retrieval
beacon announced the imminent arrival of the boat, Julian
studied his catch. These Skinnies looked older, in human
terms, than the Skinny fighting troops. They weren't in the
best shape physically; even a human eye could judge that.
And they were quiet . . . very quiet.

At last the beacon sounded. Three minutes later and right on schedule, the retrieval boat descended to land on the parking lot.

"All right, let's move 'em out. Stay behind the prisoners just in case, though," Julian ordered.

The M.I. had only twenty-five yards of open ground to cross to reach the retrieval boat. The first prisoners were herded out the doorway before the boat ramp was even down. Julian stepped out in their midst. Nothing happened.

The M.I. herded their prisoners aboard the boat.

"Made it!" Julian thought, as the retrieval boat ramp swung up. Inside the boat, the Skinny prisoners were quickly strapped down onto acceleration couches.

"Take off, pilot," Julian sang out.

I did it. I led a suicide mission and pulled it off, Julian mused as the g-force pushed his body into the padding of his couch. Got to remember about citations for some of the fellows.

Go to section 110.

— 114 —

"Antonini, deploy those listening devices! Johnson, have your squad take the right flank, here in the drop zone. Maalo, sweep left toward the big Bug hole to give cover to Antonini's men deploying the listening devices north of there."

"Julian. We're moving out now," Lieutenant Weiss called. Then he added, "Good Luck!"

"Thank you, sir."

For once, the drop had gone as planned with no hitches. The platoon had hit the drop zone dead on target. Bug missile fire had been erratic; no casualties, at least in

Julian's section. There were no signs of Bug activity on the gray, dusty surface of Birgu. Only the large, gaping holes in the ground testified to the teeming menace below.

Julian bounced due north toward the right-flank listening-post position. Want to make sure those things are set up properly, he told himself. As he moved, his tactical display showed him that Maalo and Antonini were deploying their men as ordered.

Bouncing around at forty miles per hour can be fun, Julian remembered, when there aren't Bugs shooting at you.

Julian reached the right-flank listening post in three bounces. "All in order here, sir," the private said, putting the finishing touches on his setup.

"Any noise?"

"A low steady rumble from the northwest; must be Bug traffic in that major artery."

Julian listened himself and decided the private was correct.

"Brennan here, Julian. Center listening post set up and operating."

"Good. I'll head toward the target hole. You check the left-flank post."

Once again, Julian was bounding over the barren dust, barking orders as he went and wondering why the Bugs hadn't shown themselves yet.

"Maalo, hold your position and be ready to cut down anything coming out of that hole. Johnson, form your squad in a wedge and advance on the target hole. Antonini, set up your rovers' patterns. I don't want the men at those listening posts picked off by Bugs. Take a pattern that will maximize fire support for them from known Bug hole locations. Expect them to boil out from the northwest, especially between us and the lieutenant's section."

Another scan of his tactical display showed his orders being carried out, to the letter.

"Sarge! We got Bug noises. Right-flank listening post.

There must be a trainload of them going right beneath me!''

''Maalo! Report,'' Julian snapped.

''Nothing yet, Sarge. Wait a minute. . . . Squad! Fire! We got Bugs, Sarge, lots and lots of Bugs!''

Julian already saw the Bugs emerging from the large Bug hole. Here's their reaction, he thought.

''Johnson, close to flamer range on those Bugs, fast! Maalo's too close to the hole to use grenades or rockets. Antonini, hold your position. Keep the men at those listening posts.''

Flamer fire erupted around the huge holes as a hideous black, chitinous mass emerged. Even as Julian watched, the mass began to resolve itself into individual Bugs.

There are sixteen Bugs emerging from the hole, each with an Ordnance value of 3. Only five M.I. are in range to fire at them.

The Bugs fire using Chart E.

The M.I. fire using Chart C.

After five rounds of fighting, increase M.I. Manpower by 7 to reflect the arrival of Johnson's squad along with Brennan and Julian.

Continue the fight until either all the M.I. are killed or all the Bugs are killed.

If all the Bug are killed, go to section 116.

If all the M.I. are killed, go to section 125.

— 115 —

"Julian. Fan your men out to provide rear protection for Section One. Wait until Section One has advanced about three thousand yards, then implement your plan."

"Got it, Lieutenant."

Julian bounded over the dusty, gray surface of Birgu, checking on his section and calling orders.

"Maalo, fan out far to the left, just like your were going to advance in a line heading north. Antonini, take Maalo's right flank. Johnson, form the right flank."

The drop had gone like clockwork. Bug missile fire was erratic. The section had taken no casualties coming down. And the pilot of the *Colonel Bowie* must have done something right; the drop was right on target.

Julian watched Section One advance to the northwest with the lieutenant in the lead. Then he remembered!

"Maalo! Form your squad around that big Bug hole— the one we'll be going down. Stay far enough back from it to use grenades and rockets if we need to. Antonini and Johnson, head east with squads in a single file, alternating bounces. Let's move!"

Julian himself stayed relatively stationary, gauging the advance of Section One while watching his own men on his tactical display. Section One hit the three-thousand-yard mark.

"All right! All squads, on the bounce, head for that hole. No one enters until I get there."

A scream over the comm unit nearly shattered Julian's eardrums.

"Sarge! We got Bugs!"

Julian saw laser fire erupt from the large hole, followed by a writhing, chitinous, black mass. Bugs all right, and lots of them!

"Let 'em have it!" Julian ordered.

There are sixteen Bugs coming up out of the hole, each with an Ordnance value of 3. All fifteen of Julian's men can participate in the fight.

The Bugs fire using Chart E.

The M.I. fire using Chart D.

Continue the fight until either all the Bugs or all the M.I. are killed.

If the M.I. win the fight, go to section 117.

If all the M.I. are killed, go to section 29.

— 116 —

Flames, rockets, grenade explosions, dust, and death. Those were the main things Julian remembered about the firefight. That, and the flaming bodies of the Bugs, a few of them falling back down that hole, still burning. Back down the hole he was about to enter, leading his men.

"We took care of them, all right," Brennan said.

"Right. Brennan, stay topside, assess casualties, then follow us down. We won't get too far ahead of you. Maalo, you're first man in, then me, then Johnson's squad. Johnson, as we advance, space your men at about one-thousand-yard intervals. I think the comm units will carry that far. And remember men, once we're in the tunnels, it's hand-to-hand fighting only. We'll be too close together for ranged weapons or grenades. Let's move."

Maalo led the way into the hole. Julian followed only a few feet behind him.

"We'll need to use infrared. I can't see anything ahead

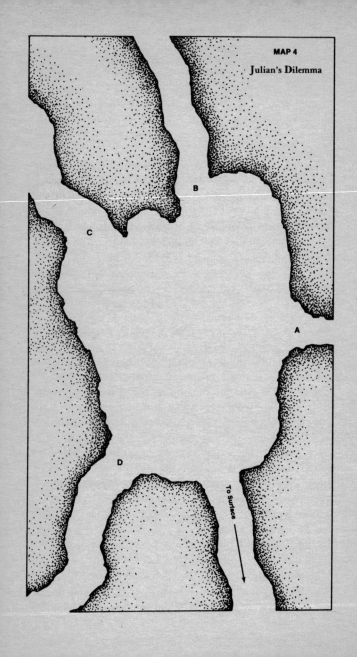

MAP 4

Julian's Dilemma

B

C

A

D

To Surface

but a few burning Bug bodies and a long, wide tunnel. Side seems kind of glazed like, and the floor is slippery,'' Maalo reported, remembering to speak in a low voice.

''Switch to infrared as you enter the hole. Walk by sliding your feet. Remember you're in powered armor. One hard step and you'll bounce up to the ceiling,'' Julian reminded his men.

The men advanced the first five hundred yards without incident. There weren't even any side tunnels. The main tunnel ran due north, as near as Julian could tell, with no twists or turns.

Just beyond the five-hundred-yard point, Julian learned why the Bug tunnels are called labyrinths. The tunnel emptied into a roughly spherical underground room. There were four other large tunnels leading out of the room, all of them heading steeply down.

''Which way, Sarge?'' whispered Maalo.

Look at Map 4. This map shows the choices facing Julian. The large tunnels leading down are marked A, B, C, and D.

If Julian chooses tunnel A, go to section 124.

If Julian chooses tunnel B, go to section 119.

If Julian chooses tunnel C, go to section 129.

If Julian chooses tunnel D, go to section 127.

— **117** —

Flames, rockets, grenade explosions, dust, and death. Those were the main things Julian remembered about the firefight. That, and the flaming bodies of the Bugs, a few of them falling back down that hole, still burning. Back down the hole he was about to enter, leading his men.

"We took care of them, all right," Brennan said.

"Right. Brennan, stay topside, assess casualties, then follow us down. We won't get too far ahead of you. Maalo, you're first man in, then me, then Johnson's squad, then Antonini's. And remember men, once we're in the tunnels, it's hand-to-hand fighting only. We'll be too close together for ranged weapons or grenades. Let's move."

Maalo led the way into the hole. Julian followed only a few feet behind him.

"We'll need to use infrared. I can't see anything ahead but a few burning Bug bodies and a long, wide tunnel. Side seems kind of glazed like, and the floor is slippery," Maalo reported, remembering to speak in a low voice.

"Switch to infrared as you enter the hole. Walk by sliding your feet. Remember you're in powered armor. One hard step and you'll bounce up to the ceiling," Julian reminded his men.

The men advanced the first five hundred yards without incident. There weren't even any side tunnels. The main tunnel ran due north, as near as Julian could tell, with no twists or turns.

Just beyond the five-hundred-yard point, Julian learned why the Bug tunnels are called labyrinths. The tunnel emptied into a roughly spherical underground room. There were four other large tunnels leading out of the room, all of them heading steeply down.

"Which way, Sarge?" whispered Maalo.

Look at Map 4. This map shows the choices facing Julian. The large tunnels leading down are marked A, B, C, and D.

If Julian chooses tunnel A, go to section 128.

If Julian chooses tunnel B, go to section 130.

If Julian chooses tunnel C, go to section 133.

If Julian chooses tunnel D, go to section 132.

— 118 —

The men performed exactly as Julian hoped. They remained in position, waited for his word, and then took off.

Julian was the first man through the tunnel entrance, and what a horrid sight greeted his eyes! Bugs, waiting for him, deployed perfectly to meet his attack. The industrial center was only two hundred yards ahead. The Bugs had even stacked equipment in the artery to use for cover. The situation couldn't be much worse.

"Kill them," Julian ordered.

There are sixteen Bugs in the large artery. Each has an Ordnance value of 3.

The M.I. fire using Chart D.

The Bugs fire using Chart E.

Continue the fight until all combatants on one side or the other are dead.

If all the M.I. are killed, go to section 29.

If all the Bugs are killed, go to section 121.

— 119 —

Go to section 122

— 120 —

"Quite a fight," Julian whispered softly. His men gazed dispassionately at the dead Bugs.

"Let's move out. Pass the word up. We're heading back to that large room, and we'll try it again from there."

Luck was with Julian as he led his men back to the large room, picked a different tunnel, and advanced again. Soon, just ahead, he saw the major Bug transport artery.

"Listen. Those Bugs were probably waiting for us right where this tunnel empties into that huge artery out there. But I'll bet that since we're still alive, they've redeployed. We'll sneak up to the mouth of the tunnel, then charge out there, hand flamers ready. There should be room to deploy up to four abreast. If you have a man behind you, fall flat and fire prone while he advances firing. Then alternate. A moving fire line, just like alternating bounces.

"Our target should be to the right. So it's sneak up, out into the artery, form a line facing right, and go to it. Got it? Let's go."

The men fell silent as they approached the tunnel mouth.

Roll the dice. If the result is the same as or less than the section's Stealth value, go to section 126.

If the result is greater than the section's Stealth value, go to section 118.

— 121 —

"Okay. We'll announce the engagement formally, but only after you're enrolled in OCS," Brenda said.

"You got it, honey."

For a while, Julian had doubted he'd ever get off Birgu. But once they got past the Bugs in the artery, it was a cakewalk. The Bugs hadn't expected raiders in their factory storage area. Aside from those warriors in the transportation artery, the place was undefended.

Julian's squad had a field day mopping up.

Now, back at Sanctuary, Sergeant Julian Penn had an application to fill out. They said OCS was tough, but Julian and Brenda thought he had the stuff to make it.

THE END

— 122 —

Maalo led the squad down the tunnel chosen by Julian. The tunnel began to wind around until it was impossible to maintain an accurate sense of direction.

"Something ahead, Sarge," Maalo called softly.

Julian peered forward. A large cavernlike room loomed ahead with no tunnels leading out. Dead end!

"Sarge, message from the surface. Listening post on the right flank reports a 'frying bacon' sound just south of them."

Bugs! They're cutting in behind us! Julian realized the situation was desperate. The men had hit a dead end, Bugs were closing in from behind, and there was no place that provided suitable cover.

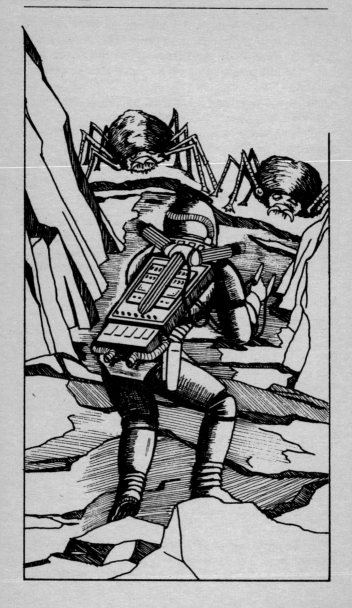

Quickly, Julian deployed his men in the large room. Two went on either side of the entrance. They would fire flamers at dangerously close range as the Bugs came at them. The rest hung back, ready to join the melee at the doorway.

"All men strung along the tunnels, try to hide, let them pass. We'll take them," Julian ordered.

He didn't have long to wait. Through some alien sense of direction, the Bugs headed right for them.

"Here they come, Sarge," called the nervous private to the left of the doorway.

"Fire," Julian ordered calmly.

There are sixteen Bugs with a Melee value of 4 each. There are only six M.I. The rest are strung back along the tunnels. Only two M.I. can fire in the first round of the fight. The bugs do not fight back in the first round. The second and all succeeding rounds are melee.

The M.I. fire using Chart A.

The M.I. melee using Chart D.

The Bugs melee using Chart E.

If all the M.I. are killed, go to section 29.

If all the Bugs are killed, go to section 120.

— **123** —

The fight ended quickly. Julian sized up his losses, then pressed on.

"Let's move quickly. The Bugs in the tunnel mouth will

probably redeploy now that their plan has gone awry. If we hurry, we may catch them in the act.''

Julian moved as rapidly as possible down the tunnel, praying for a glimpse of that major artery. Soon, he spotted it.

''Okay, this is it. Move up as quietly as possible, then into that artery, turn right, and advance flaming away. The artery looks wide enough for us to go four abreast. Men in front line down, alternating fire with those in back, then those in back advance, forming moving lines with continuous firing. Got it? Let's go!''

Roll two dice. If the result is equal to or less than the section's Stealth value, go to section 126.

If the result of the roll is higher than the section's Stealth value, go to section 118.

— 124 —

Go to section 122.

— 125 —

Maalo's men fought well, but went down fast. The Bugs cut up Johnson's squad as soon as they closed, but Julian managed to radio Lieutenant Weiss before he died. The M.I. under Weiss stabilized the situation, but the war was over for Julian's section.

Go to section 29.

— 126 —

The men performed exactly as Julian hoped. They remained in position, waited for his word, and then took off.

Julian was the first man through the tunnel entrance, and what a glorious sight greeted his eyes! Bugs with their backs to him, redeploying toward the industrial center only two hundred yards ahead. Plenty of room to use flamers, and good range as well. The situation couldn't have been much better, unless he was safe in a bunk.

"We did it! Let's get them!" Julian cried.

There are sixteen Bugs in the large artery. Each has an Ordnance value of 3.

The M.I. have achieved surprise. The Bugs do not fire in the first round of the fight.

The M.I. fire using Chart A.

The Bugs fire using Chart E.

Continue the fight until all combatants on one side or the other are dead.

If all the M.I. are killed, go to section 29.

If all the Bugs are killed, go to section 121.

— 127 —

Go to section 122.

— 128 —

Go to section 131.

— 129 —

After that first large room, there were several other side corridors, but all were smaller than the one the men followed. Julian decided to push ahead in the larger tunnel, reasoning that it would probably intersect the major transport artery leading to the industrial facility.

As they advanced, Julian tried to keep track of the distance and the bearing in his own mind. A difficult task. At the moment, he thought the men were heading northwest, just passing under the right-flank listening post above. That meant the Bug artery should be about fifteen hundred yards ahead.

"Sarge, message from the surface. Antonini reports that the lieutenant and Section One are heavily engaged against a horde of bugs far to the northwest, near the Bug hole concentration. Also, the right-flank listening post reports a funny sound coming from due south of it. They say it sounds like frying bacon."

Bugs! Julian thought. They're coming in behind us, probably planning to hit us from behind when we move from this tunnel into that major artery. Sure. Makes sense. There'll be more waiting at the artery entrance, too.

Julian quickly surveyed the situation. His portion of the tunnel was honeycombed with entrances to smaller side tunnels.

"All right," Julian said in a low, calm voice. "We're going to have company. I want every man to duck into a side tunnel, take cover, and be ready for a Bug attack coming down from our rear. We'll have to take the blasted things hand to hand. Now, scatter! And stay quiet!''

The six men still with Julian quietly glided into side corridor entrances. No one spoke. Julian learned the loudest sound in the world was the beating of his own heart.

They waited, and waited, and waited. After two minutes, which seemed like forever, they heard the scuttling sound of Bugs coming down the tunnel.

"Wait for my signal, then jump them," Julian ordered, very quietly.

The Bugs came scuttling along two abreast, moving rapidly. The first two Bugs passed the first two M.I. before they even started to slow down.

"Now, hit 'em!" Julian called.

There are sixteen Bugs in the melee, each with a Melee value of 4. Julian has a total of six M.I. present to fight.

The M.I. get two rounds of free attacks, reflecting the Bugs' surprise.

The Bugs fight using Chart E, beginning in the third round.

The M.I. fight using Chart C.

Continue the fight until all the Bugs or all the M.I. are killed.

If all the M.I. are killed, go to section 29.

If all the Bugs are killed, go to section 123.

— 130 —

Go to section 131.

— 131 —

Maalo led the squad down the tunnel chosen by Julian. The tunnel began to wind around until it was impossible to maintain an accurate sense of direction.

"Something ahead, Sarge," Maalo called softly.

Julian peered forward. A large cavernlike room loomed ahead with no tunnels leading out. Dead end!

Antonini's voice boomed in Julian's ears.

"Bugs, Sarge, right behind us and coming fast. What do we do?"

Bugs! They're cutting in behind us! Julian realized the situation was desperate. The men had hit a dead end, Bugs were closing in from behind, and there was no place that provided suitable cover.

Julian tried to deploy his men in the large room, but there was no time. The Bugs were on them, swarming everywhere at once.

There are sixteen Bugs with a Melee value of 4 each.

The M.I. melee using Chart D.

The Bugs melee using Chart E.

The Bugs get two free rounds of attack because the M.I. are surprised. The M.I. begin fighting back on the third round.

© 1986

If all the M.I. are killed, go to section 29.

If all the Bugs are killed, go to section 134.

— 132 —

Go to section 131.

— 133 —

After that first large room, there were several other side corridors, but all were smaller than the one the men followed. Julian decided to push ahead in the larger tunnel, reasoning that it would probably intersect the major transport artery leading to the industrial facility.

As they advanced, Julian tried to keep track of the distance and the bearing in his own mind. A difficult task. At the moment, he thought the men were heading northwest. The Bug transportation artery should be about fifteen hundred yards ahead.

"Aaaahh!"

The scream drowned out all other sounds, ringing in Julian's ears. Then he heard Antonini calling.

"Sarge, Bugs! They're taking us from the rear!"

Julian whirled and saw the Bugs already scrambling over his rearmost men, more than he could count and coming fast. There are probably more waiting at the tunnel mouth ahead, Julian thought.

There are sixteen bugs in the melee, each with a Melee

value of 4. Julian has all the remaining M.I. present to fight.

The Bugs fight using Chart E.

The M.I. fight using Chart C.

The Bugs get two rounds of free attacks, reflecting the M.I.'s surprise.

Continue the fight until all the Bugs or all the M.I. are killed.

If all the M.I. are killed, go to section 29.

If all the Bugs are killed, go to section 94.

— 134 —

"Quite a fight," Julian whispered softly. His men gazed dispassionately at the dead Bugs.

"Let's move out. We're heading back to that large room, and we'll try it again from there."

Luck was with Julian as he led his men back to the large room, picked a different tunnel, and advanced again. Soon, just ahead, he saw the major Bug transport artery.

"Listen. The Bugs were probably waiting for us right where this tunnel empties into that huge artery out there. But I'll bet that since we're still alive, they've redeployed. We'll sneak up to the mouth of the tunnel, then charge out there, hand flamers ready. There should be room to deploy up to four abreast. If you have a man behind you, fall flat and fire prone while he advances firing. Then alternate. A moving fire line, just like alternating bounces.

"Our target should be to the right. So it's sneak up, out

into the artery, form a line facing right, and go to it. Got it? Let's go.''

The men fell silent as they approached the tunnel mouth.

Roll two dice. If the result is the same as or less than the section's Stealth value, go to section 126.

If the result of the roll is greater than the section's Stealth value, go to section 118.

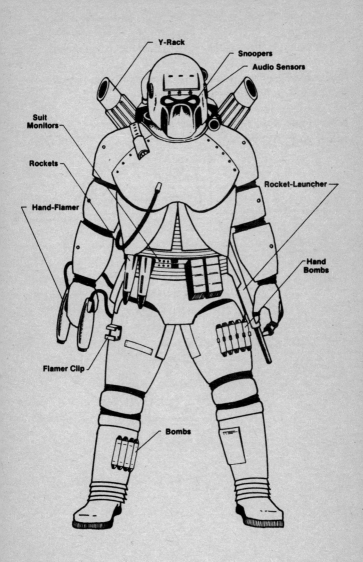

Y-Rack

Snoopers

Audio Sensors

Suit Monitors

Rockets

Hand-Flamer

Rocket-Launcher

Hand Bombs

Flamer Clip

Bombs

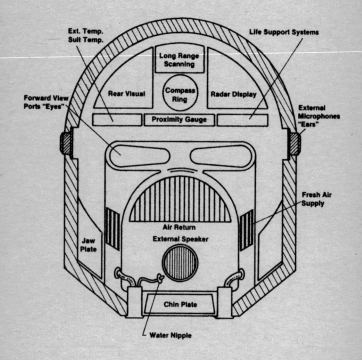

Ext. Temp.
Suit Temp.

Life Support Systems

Long Range
Scanning

Compass
Ring

Forward View
Ports "Eyes"

Rear Visual

Radar Display

Proximity Gauge

External
Microphones
"Ears"

Air Return

Fresh Air
Supply

Jaw
Plate

External Speaker

Chin Plate

Water Nipple

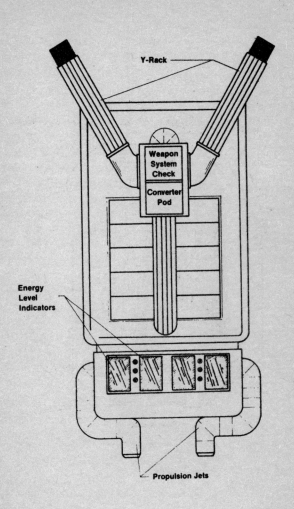

Y-Rack

Weapon
System
Check

Converter
Pod

Energy
Level
Indicators

Propulsion Jets

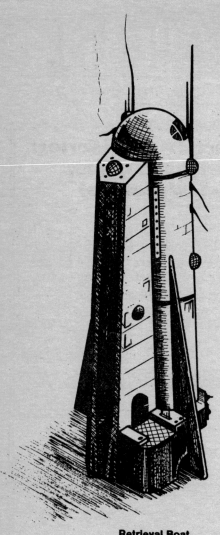

Retrieval Boat